Twists, Turns and 100% Tilda

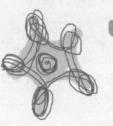

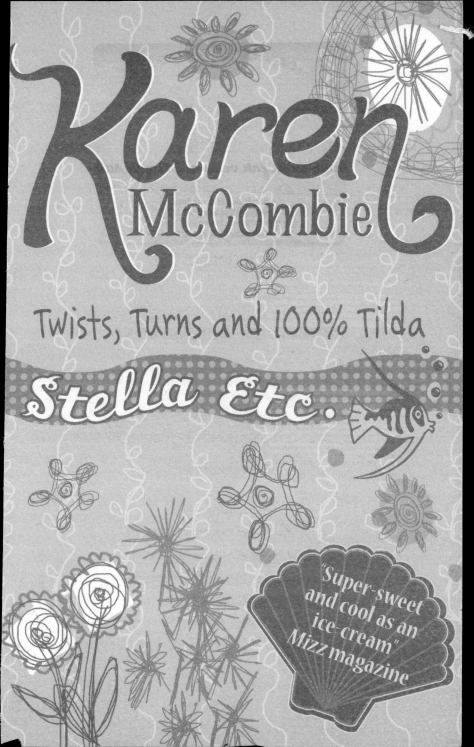

Karen McCombie

Twists, Turns and 100% Tilda

Stella Etc.

"Super-sweet and cool as an ice-cream"
Mizz magazine

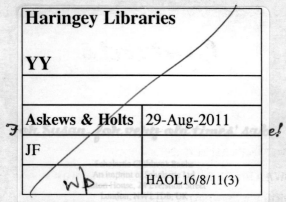

Registered office: Westfield Road, Southam, Warwickshire, CV47 0RA

First published in the UK by Scholastic Ltd, 2006
This edition published in the UK by Scholastic Ltd, 2011

ISBN 9781407124179

A CIP catalogue record for this book is available from the British Library.

Printed in the UK by CPI Bookmarque, Croydon, Surrey.
Papers used by Scholastic Children's Books are made from wood grown in
sustainable forests.

1 3 5 7 9 10 8 6 4 2

This is a work of fiction. Names, characters, places, incidents and dialogues are products of the
author's imagination or are used fictitiously. Any resemblance to actual people, living or dead,
events or locales is entirely coincidental.

www.scholastic.co.uk/zone

Contents

From: *stella*
To: Frankie
Subject: Full-on nuts-ness!
Attachments: Twists, Turns & 100% Tilda

Hi Frankie!

Ha – so, you said in your last e-mail that you're "enjoying" being back at school after the holidays. I'm sure all the teachers would be deeply thrilled to know you added "as much as having my eyebrows shaved off".

Can you believe that once upon a time *I* was stressing out so much about starting school here in Portbay? And so far this first week's been OK! (Well, I *did* stress a little bit when I got muddled up and walked into the staff room instead of the loos…)

Anyway, the reason starting school seems such a breeze is because the week before this, everything was completely, full-on *NUTS* – with a whole lot of spooky thrown in too.

With everything going on, it's been hard to explain every mad twist and turn to you properly, so here's the full, detailed, *splurged* version, on the attached document. Hope it doesn't fry your brain!

1

Miss you ☹, but M8s 4eva ☺!

stella

PS Counting off the days till it's half-term and I can come and see you and the gang again. Promise I won't take Peaches – I'd get too many weird looks on the train for having an enormo, scruffy cat taking up a whole seat-and-a-half...

Chapter 1

Never wear ice cream near a dog. . .

"Big Banana!" I yelled, stepping out of the kitchen into the garden and the bright, white midday sunshine.

I wasn't insulting my friend TJ, by the way – just trying to get him to choose a flavour of ice cream.

Holding the tray, I squinted into the sharp light and waited for an answer. As my eyes adjusted to the brightness, all I could make out were two eerily greeny-blue dragonflies swirling in a sort of slow waltz over the centre of the garden.

Being temporarily blinded, I didn't know if TJ could see me clearly or not. I hoped he coudn't – or at least, I hoped my cheeks weren't still telltale red. I hated the idea of TJ spotting that I was blushing and asking what was up. I mean, how could I explain that five minutes ago, my stupid brain had just had a flashback? A flashback to the (urgh) Emergency Kiss?

3

Oh yes – *that*.

Four weeks ago, I did something *seriously* freaky. I had an Emergency Kiss with my best (boy) mate – and I'd tried to forget about it ever since.

Then there I am, ambling around my kitchen, thinking about ice cream when *blam!* it plops unannounced into my memory banks. How come? Well, the electrons or electrodes or electro-whatevers that make your brain work went on a mad meander right after I'd clocked a newspaper cutting Blu-tacked to the fridge door. Mum must have put it there – it was about the fund-raising campaign she'd come up with.

So how did my brain get from a story in the local paper to the Emergency Kiss? *This* is how…

Sponsor a Crystal campaign → the grand chandelier in the old derelict mansion in Sugar Bay (Joseph's house) → how to save it before Joseph's house got demolished → stumbling on a gang who were vandalizing the place → spotting the police coming and panicking that they might think me and TJ were part of the gang → pretending to be a loved-up couple instead → having an EMERGENCY KISS so we looked convincing!!

Urgh…

Before I'd made it back out into the garden, I'd had to stick my face in the cool of the freezer to blast away the blushes, and hummed a rude version of "Twinkle Twinkle Little Star" (taught to me by my friend Frankie back in London) to help nudge thoughts of the Emergency Kiss to the back of my overactive mind.

"Big Banana?" I tried calling out again.

There was no answer from TJ.

"Or what about Cherry Berry, then? I got vanilla for Bob…"

My witterings about ice cream were met by more silence. (Well, apart from the hammering and crashing coming from my bedroom upstairs.)

OK…

I gazed around our madly overgrown back garden, but all I could see was thigh-high grass and weeds.

I glanced over at the den (a little brick outhouse that was mine, all mine), but the latch was still on.

I frowned at the path that led down the side of the house, but couldn't imagine that TJ and Bob would just take off without saying bye – specially not when I'd promised TJ there was ice cream in the freezer.

Hmm. TJ and his bear-sized, long-haired Alsatian had disappeared. I'd only been gone five

5

minutes, and our mutant garden had swallowed them. Lurking under all the tangle was probably a large, bottomless pit that my family had no idea existed.

"*LOCAL TEENAGER VANISHES*," the headline would read in the *Portbay Journal*. "*The son of well-known drama teacher Caroline O'Connell, thirteen-year-old Titus, vanished with his dog while visiting the home of a friend…*"

Stop right there – I *had* to find him. There was no way I'd risk TJ's real name being found out by the whole town. (Mrs O'Connell must've referred to him as "Titus" at Parents' Evenings, but obviously the teachers at school felt sorry enough for him to respect his choice and call him TJ too.)

"TJ!" I said urgently.

Nothing.

Nothing apart from the two dragonflies stopping stock-still in the air at the sound of my voice.

"*TJ!!*" I yelled louder, feeling a little spooked.

"Wuff!" barked Bob, from somewhere in the dense undergrowth.

The dragonflies shot upwards in fright and carried on their circling waltz from a safer height.

"What?!" said TJ, popping his head above the long grass like a skater-boy jack-in-the-box.

I saw he had his headphones in. He'd been too busy nodding along to his newest favourite band to listen out for me coming back from the kitchen. But what was he (and his dumb dog) doing in the the middle of our private jungle-cum-prairie?

"Great – what've you got, Stella?" asked TJ, standing up now and flipping the headphones into the palm of one hand.

"Um, two juices, a bowl of water, three bowls of ice cream and some hairclips," I said, reeling off everything that was on the tray I was carrying. "What are you doing over there, TJ?"

"Making a crop circle!" TJ grinned, ushering me to join him with a sweep of his arm.

"A *what*-ty?" I asked automatically, holding the tray up as I waded through the scratchy long grasses.

I knew what he meant: fields full of wheat or whatever, with parts flattened into intricate swirly patterns. You saw them in the newspapers now and then, with stories about how they must be made by aliens. My grandad (Grandad Stansfield, who lives in the country) says they're nothing to do with aliens – just guys going out armed with long planks of wood (for flattening purposes) to play a giant-sized practical joke on the rest of us.

Yep, so I got all that. I just didn't get why TJ was

talking about them – till I found myself stepping into a metre-and-a-half wide island of squashed-flat foliage.

"Well, I stood in what I reckoned was the middle of your garden, lay right down, and then sort of *walked* my legs around in a circle till it ended up like this!" TJ explained, flopping himself down beside Bob.

I joined them, plonking the tray in the middle of our hidden oasis.

"It's like a mini lawn!" I smiled, enjoying having somewhere to sit in the garden at last.

"With walls!" TJ joked, pointing to the banks of grasses surrounding our secret world.

As if his entrance had just been announced, Peaches chose that second to wriggle his fat, ginger cattiness through the wall of greenery and join us.

"Hey, Peaches! Welcome to our secret world!" said TJ, while I reached over and scratched his head, and Bob cowered a little. (Bob knew who was boss out of him and Peaches; i.e. it wasn't Bob.)

"So, anyway, what flavour ice cream are these, Stella?" asked TJ, getting back to business now that Peaches had flopped himself into a comfy pile of fur against my legs, his emerald eyes fixed on the bright greeny-blue dragonflies above us.

"Big Banana and Cherry Berry," I repeated, placing the bowl of water and the vanilla ice cream in front of a panting Bob. "Which do you want?"

"Don't mind. *You* choose," said TJ, proving why I liked him. *I* knew that *he* knew that we both liked Big Banana best.

"I choose ... that we eat half a bowl each and then swap," I suggested, hoping I seemed like just as good a friend.

"Done." TJ grinned, getting stuck right in.

I started on mine a few seconds later, once I'd snapped a couple of my spangly hairclips on to Bob's face fur. As soon as the floppiness was pinned back, he looked instantly cooler, and the fluoro pink stars matched his lolling pink tongue very nicely.

"So ... what's your dad actually doing in there?" asked TJ, nodding up at my room, right above the kitchen extension.

"Redecorating."

"With a *hammer*?"

I didn't bother replying – just rolled my eyes instead. On the one hand, I was very grateful that Dad had offered to fix up my decrepit room, and on the other hand ... well, listening to the banging, crashing and occasional swearing drifting out of the window, it kept reminding me that he wasn't exactly a natural-born DIY-er.

"I thought I'd stop working on the rest of the house and get your room together, Stella, since school starts in a week," Dad had explained over a family fish'n'chips tea on the beach last night, "and you'll need somewhere nice and calm to do your homework."

Hmm ... somewhere nice and calm to do my homework – away from my rampaging two-year-old brothers, he meant.

And more importantly, hmm ... starting at a new school. I'd been doing really well at putting *that* to the back of my mind lately. I'd been too busy getting used to my new home town of Portbay (and all its weirdness) to get my head around stuff like new schools. But at least I knew I had TJ – and Rachel – in my year. Amber would be around too, even though I wouldn't see that much of her, since she was fifteen and a couple of years above us.

Still, what was the point in worrying about that now? School was nine days away, and since I'd been in Portbay, I'd found out that a whole lot of *everything* can happen in *one* day, never mind nine...

"Swap!" announced TJ, holding out his bowl of

gently melting pinky-purple ice cream.

"So ... what should we do today?" I asked, passing him my gorgeous banana and fudge gloop.

"Dunno. D'you want to go back to Pavilion Park and take a photo of the bench?"

I know, I *know* ... taking a photo of a bench doesn't sound like any big wow unless that dull little park bench happens to have an inscription on it that *blows your mind*.

"Yeah – *that* would be good." I nodded. "How did it go again? Oh, I know... '*In memory of my grandfather, Joe Grainger, who loved to sit on this spot and gaze at the sea, and think of his faraway home.*' It's kind of beautiful and tragic, isn't it? The idea of this old man sitting looking out to sea, thinking about Barbados..."

Barbados was the connection I had with the long ago, long-since-dead Joseph (yeah, the Joseph from Joseph's house). I'd never been to Barbados, but a quarter of me was Barbadian, thanks to my grandad Eddie, who I'd never met. Actually, that's as far as the connection went. After all, Joseph had sailed to Portbay from Barbados as a ten-year-old servant boy nearly two hundred years ago, while *I*, er, drove in my family car to Portbay from London, as a grumbling, complaining thirteen-year-old all of five weeks ago...

"Yeah, well, the most tragic thing about it," said TJ, putting down his bowl now he'd scraped every last dribble of ice cream off it, "is that Joseph was obviously *rubbish* at geography. He was looking in completely the wrong direction – Barbados is *that* way!"

Trust a boy to spoil a romantic idea with boring practical facts. I was toying with splatting my last spoonful of Cherry Berry in his face when my mobile burst into life.

"Stella? It's me."

I was tempted to say "Who?", just to be awkward, but settled for "Hi, Rach," instead.

At the sound of Rachel's name, TJ pulled a face. It had been a while since Rachel swapped from being an enemy to a friend of TJ's, but I guess old habits die hard.

Anyway, spotting that I was distracted with the phone call, TJ cheekily leant over and grabbed my wrist, turning the spoon towards his mouth.

"Listen – a couple of things," said Rachel, unaware of the wrestling match currently going on between me and TJ (he was *not* having that last dollop of ice cream). "First, Mum's sold all of the fairy pictures you and TJ did. She's got fifty quid for each of you and says you can collect it any time."

Fifty quid?! Me and TJ had done the fake fairy project for fun, sticking my fairy paintings around the prettily tangled gardens at Joseph's house and snapping them. Now, the prints that Mrs Riley had framed and stuck in the window of her arty-crafty souvenir shop had actually made us money. Quite a *lot* of money. The electro-wotsits in my brain whirred into action again, working out what I might be able to buy with fifty pounds.

a) a pair of new expensive trainers

OR

b) lots of clothes if I went to the bargainously cheap store in Westbay shopping centre

OR

c) a whole bunch of new art paper and paints and stuff

OR

d) I could give the whole fifty pounds to the Sponsor a Crystal campaign.

Well, it was going to have to be d).

My last pair of trainers weren't too scruffy yet; I had lots of clothes already; I had enough art stuff to last me a while longer ... but time was running out to save the chandelier and get it moved to the town's museum before the developers came along to smash the house – and everything that was left in it – to pieces.

"And another thing," Rachel chatted in my ear, as me and TJ carried on wrestling with the spoon. "You have GOT to come down to the prom right now – I'm in Mum's shop, and I can see a whole crew of the cutest surfer boys setting up down on the beach!"

"Really?"

"*Really!*" said Rachel emphatically.

Distracted by the thought of cute surfer boys clogging up the sands and waves with their boards and nice muscles, I lost my concentration and let go of the spoon. Oops.

Melted ice cream sprayed over TJ's face, like splatters of strange, dark pink freckles. One dollop in particular dangled from his nose, threatening to drip. TJ stuck out his tongue, just in time to catch it.

"Yay! *I* got the last of the ice cream! *I* got the last of the ice cream!" he sing-songed. "*I* got the last of the – oof, *yuck*!! NOOOOO!"

"What's going on?" asked Rachel, catching some of the racket TJ was making.

"He's being eaten by Bob," I told her, watching as a writhing TJ (quite small for his age) was pinned to the ground by his dog (enormously huge for a pooch).

This was good: for *me*, obviously, not for TJ. *Now* any time that yukky thoughts of Emergency

Kisses pinged uninvited into my head, I could just banish them by thinking of TJ being unexpectedly and unattractively licked to death by a slobbering Alsatian.

"Help get him off me, Stella!" TJ begged, as he struggled and giggled under the mighty, determined tongue of Bob.

There was no point shouting at Bob – he never listened to anyone except TJ. There was no point pulling at his collar – it would be like a wasp tugging at a rhinoceros. There was no point trying to tempt him away with food – all the ice cream, apart from the splatters on TJ's face, was gone. But I *did* have a secret weapon…

Quickly, I scooped up a lumpy, heavy pile of fluff (i.e. Peaches), then manoeuvred us both around so that Peaches was gazing directly at Bob, their noses just centimetres apart.

It did the trick, of course.

There was no hissing, spitting or scratching. The silent, piercing, neon-green-eyed stare of my weirdy cat was enough to shock Bob into stopping dead in his licking tracks, and make him reverse speedily into the very "wall" of the grassy oasis.

"Thanks, Stella!" TJ panted, sitting up and wiping his face on the bottom of his T-shirt. "You're a star!"

Stella the star?

Actually, it was more a case of Stella the Desperate – desperate to get down to the beach as quickly as possible.

The unfurling mystery of Joseph had been around for nearly a couple of centuries so far – *surely* I could take a couple of hours off thinking about it to go nosey at those cute teen surfer boys that Rachel mentioned…?

Chapter 2

How not to sound pathetic and shallow (please)

"Hurdles?"

"No."

"Cross-country running?"

"No."

"Synchronized swimming?"

"No."

"Rhythmic gymnastics?"

"What's that again?" I asked, trying to remember if it had something potentially painful to do with parallel bars or not.

"Girls in leotards jumping with big ribbons," said TJ, clearing up the confusion for me.

"Well, then, no."

"Netball?"

"No."

"Basketball?"

"No."

"Volleyball?"

"No."

17

"Ping-pong?"

"No."

Those were just a *few* of the sports that TJ had been naming as we walked at high speed down towards the beach. And every single sport that he'd mentioned so far I had either a) never tried, b) never been any good at, or c) never been particularly interested in (probably because I knew I'd be rubbish at them).

Anyway, why was TJ pestering me with a list of sports and asking if I liked them? What was his point exactly? I hadn't a clue. OK, I had – I knew it was the beginning of some kind of wind-up at my expense.

"So, Stella ... out of *all* of those, there're *none* that you're particularly fussed about."

"Like, I said, nope." I shrugged, as the three of us (Bob included) stopped at the pavement on the prom, and looked from side to side for an opening in the holidaymaking traffic. And there was one now – TJ scooped a hand under Bob's collar as we darted across the road.

"Well, if you're not that fussed about *any* sport," said TJ over his shoulder, landing on the opposite pavement a footfall before me, thanks to being dragged there by Bob, "then how come we've *rushed* down here to see some lads surfing?"

"*Because*..." I began, feeling my cheeks start to redden.

Help. What was I going to say next? I didn't want to sound pathetic and shallow and admit it was just 'cause Rachel told me on the phone that they were cute. But suddenly I knew TJ had sussed that out already: cue the wind-up.

"Hey, check this out!" muttered TJ, stopping so quickly that me and Bob carried on along the pavement. (Oh deep joy – something had distracted TJ. I could stop my mind whirring in a panic, uselessly trying to find something to add to that "because...".)

"What is it?" I asked, backtracking a few steps.

TJ was staring at an A4 sheet of crumpled white paper taped to one of the old-fashioned blue-painted lamp-posts that were dotted along the prom.

I joined in with the staring. If you crossed your eyes, you might have thought you were looking at a letter, but when you read it properly – eyes in their normal positions – you couldn't. Read it, I mean. That's 'cause it wasn't written in any language I recognized, and growing up in inner-city London, I've seen a *lot*. This wasn't the quirky Greek alphabet, or the boxy Russian alphabet, or even the squiggly, wriggly Ethiopian alphabet. It

19

wasn't swirly Turkish, or even *more* swirly Arabic. It was just a bunch of small squares, triangles and circles, with random, added dots and slashes here and there.

"Y'know, I've seen a couple of these pinned up round town lately," said TJ, turning his head sideways, like that would help him read what it said (don't think it did).

"What are you two doing?" asked a voice that was faintly lispy and very blunt all at the same time.

It was Rachel Riley, officially the prettiest teenager in Portbay – if you happen to think that girls who look like bored Siamese cats are pretty, and most people do seem to, specially *boy* people.

"Well, we're busy *not* being able to read this," TJ told Rachel, as he pointed up at the note. "Would you like to *not* read it with us?"

"TJ, *why* do you always have to come out with dumb things?" Rachel frowned at him, before fixing her gaze on the note and frowning even more.

Rachel sometimes seemed as though she'd had a sense of humour bypass – probably because until very recently she'd hung out with her old friends, Kayleigh and co, whose hobbies seemed to be snarling and being sarky. But since she'd been mates with me and TJ, she'd shown definite signs of improvement. Though maybe not right at this second.

"TJ says he's seen a few of these around – have you, Rach?" I asked her.

"No. What's it supposed to be? Ancient Egyptian or something?"

"It's not any language we know," TJ suddenly muttered darkly. "Which kind of fits in with what some people round here have been saying lately…"

"What?" I nearly asked, before I felt his elbow nudge mine just the *tiniest* bit. (I couldn't figure out what he was up to – but that nudge made me shut up anyway.)

"What are people saying?" asked Rachel, intrigued.

"Well, first they tried to contact us through corn circles…"

"*They*? They who?" Rachel butted in. "What people?"

"Not people – aliens."

For a split second, Rachel looked slightly spooked. The mug.

"And *now* they're trying to reach us with their strange messages," TJ added, nodding knowingly, and tapping at the taped-on sheet of A4.

"Huh?" mumbled Rachel, gazing from the "message" to TJ and back again, her eyes narrowed but her expression saying "gullible".

"Oh, yes. And if they can't get through to us *that* way," TJ wittered on, "they'll probably try putting an ad in the newsagent's window. Y'know: *Alien – tall, weird, one-eyed, looking for friendship with human, possibly leading to romance.*"

"Ha ha *ha*," growled Rachel, snapping back to her cynical self. "Zero out of ten for *that* joke, TJ. Anyway, Stella, are you coming to check out these surfer lads or not? Amber's on her lunch-break – she's nabbed a good spot down on the sand."

"'*Checking them out*', eh?" TJ grinned, ignoring Rachel ignoring him and letting go of Bob's collar so he could lollop off, fur flying, starry hairclips twinkling in the sun.

"Mmm," I muttered, shielding my eyes with my hands and seeing no one in the sea yet apart from a few splashing kids and some paddling OAPs.

"So, would that be 'checking out' the surfers' *skill*, then, Stella? Up for seeing a few carves and cutbacks?"

"Huh? Since when did you know all about surfing, TJ?" I asked, impressed with his techno-speak (and desperate to avoid the follow-up wind-up I sensed looming).

"Look, I've watched *plenty* of surfing movies when I should've been doing homework…"

"You saddo, TJ," teased Rachel, as the three of us stomped and slithered along the golden sands. "Anyway, have you spotted Amber yet? She's still looking pretty good today, even if she's back wearing that rotten waitress get-up…"

We could see that Bob had already had a close-up look at Amber, making her giggle as he bounded over to her on the beach and sniffed hopefully at her sandwich.

From the quick glimpses I could get of her – 'cause of Bob bounding about in the way – Amber *did* look pretty good. Well, as good as you can in an outfit that's made for someone with a figure that's the exact opposite to yours. (The last waitress who worked at the café must have been as short and wide as Amber was skinny and tall.)

Still, the two obvious differences were that Amber was wearing her red hair all soft and loose, instead of wrapped up in her usual ratty, tangly pair of plaits. And the other difference was that she was smiling and looked sort of … *relaxed*. Until yesterday, all I'd ever seen of Amber was this lanky, awkward girl who tried to fold herself up origami-style till she practically disappeared.

(Hey, maybe Origami Girl could be in the next instalment of the *X-Men*...?)

So something had changed. But what? I guess having Si Riley – Rachel's wow-ish older brother – offer to be your date at a naff family wedding would help a girl's confidence. Plus Rachel, me and TJ had done an amazing make-under on Amber yesterday – a task that wasn't too easy, considering her hairdresser mum had styled her like someone you snigger at off ancient pop videos on those *I ♥ the 80s* shows.

"Grab a seat!" Amber called out to us, pointing to the bum-shaped semicircles she'd scooped out in the sand next to her. "They've just finished waxing their boards!"

"Oh, no! Did I miss them changing into their wetsuits?" Rachel said in alarm, staring at the dozen or so lads down by the water's edge.

"Yep. While you were on the prom looking for Stella and TJ," Amber told her, as she fed chunks of sandwich to a forever grateful (i.e. forever hungry) Bob.

"Who are these guys, anyway?" I asked, as Rachel sighed like a deflating party balloon. "I haven't seen surfers here before..."

"A few of them came into the café earlier," said Amber. "They're all from Cornwall, but they're spending their summer holidays working their way round lots of different beaches to try out the waves."

Funny ... in London, I'd thought waves were the same wherever, like the wind was the wind, and clouds were clouds, but I was obviously wrong.

"Oh," started Amber, something pinging into her head. "You missed your mum too, Rach – she came over from the shop and gave me this... She said you left it behind."

Rachel looked at her mobile like it was a stray mouldy sock.

"She only wants me to have it so she can keep track of me *all* the time," Rachel groaned. "Why can't she leave me alone?"

"Er ... because you've just had two epileptic seizures out of the blue?" I suggested.

I understood how claustrophobic it must've been for Rachel to have her mum asking how she was feeling every five seconds (or more), but it was *hardly* a big surprise, considering.

"Ah, but I haven't *just* had them, have I?! That's the point!"

Me, Amber and TJ stayed quiet for a millisecond, each of us wondering if any of the others understood what Rachel meant. It didn't seem like it.

"Look, OK – so I had two seizures close together," said Rachel, with slight annoyance in her voice at having to explain herself to her idiot mates. "But I haven't had any more in three weeks – and I feel fine. Maybe it was just a one-off!"

"A *two*-off, you mean…" TJ corrected her, earning a dagger-eyed look for his trouble.

Hmm. It didn't seem like a good time to mention that Rachel's weird side effects were still happening. I didn't think for a second that there were too many other epileptics around who'd turned slightly psychic after the electro-wotsits in their brains overloaded and brought on seizures, but that's exactly what had happened to Rachel. Once the scariness of the seizures was over, a reluctant Rachel was left with a touch of second sight here and there. ("What's so good about knowing what ad's going to come on telly next or the exact second your dad's going to sneeze?" she moaned after the first couple of times it happened, wishing, I guess, that she was just a normal, non-epileptic, non-psychic teenager.)

"Woah – look, look, look! Gorgeous boys hurling themselves into the sea!" Amber announced hurriedly, wafting what was left of her sandwich towards the waves.

TJ immediately broke into some excellent

comedy snoring, nearly drowning out the sound of an incoming text to my mobile.

"Who's it from?" he asked, understandably more interested in my message than in ogling at surf-dudes.

"Megan – it's from Megan!" I said, pleased to hear from the long-lost member of our crew.

OK, so Megan was about as long-lost as Rachel's seizures were – she'd only been gone a week and a bit; gone back to her home after what turned out to be a slightly deranged family holiday here in Portbay.

"What's she saying?"

"Um, nothing much," I mumbled to TJ, scrolling down and skimming the words. "She just wants my home number. Wonder why?"

As I zapped my number in, with a "why?" tucked at the end, I heard TJ mumbling something too.

"What's *their* problem?"

"Whose?" I asked, glancing up as I pressed the send button to see the surf boys sniggering at something, or should I say *someone*.

"I guess their problem is that they probably don't see too many mental goth ballerinas strolling along the beaches where they usually surf," Rachel said dryly.

She was talking about Tilda Gilmore. *Yeah*, so she was wearing her usual uniform of black leather jacket, pink tutu, stripy tights and big chunky boots, and *yeah*, it was one of the hottest days of the summer so far, but so what? She was just being a hundred percent herself, and *no one* had any right to take the mick so obviously.

"What's it got to do with them, how she looks, I mean?" I said out loud, thinking that some of the lardier, less fit surfer boys looked a bit like a cross between stranded seals and half-baked bread rolls in their cut-off rubber wetsuits.

Instead of being intrigued by this gang of lads, I suddenly resented them for turning up on *our* beach and sniggering at someone who lived here, even if that someone *did* dress ... a little oddly.

"Says the queen of style, with her one hairy ginger leg!" Rachel suddenly started giggling at me.

"Huh?"

"Oh, yeah!" TJ snorted. "What's with *that*, Stella? Are you turning into a mutant werewolf? Or did the aliens abduct you while you were sleeping and carry out some evil experiment on you?"

Glancing down, I saw what my friends (and probably everyone I'd passed on the way down here) had spotted. I had one normal, light brown-skinned leg, and one hairy ginger one – thanks to slapping on suntan lotion two minutes before Peaches fell asleep on my leg back in the garden.

"Go in the sea and wash it off, Stella," Amber suggested kindly.

"Or you *could* get Bob to roll on your other leg, so they match – sort of!" TJ offered, not so kindly.

"Yeah, yeah," I managed to laugh, pushing myself up on to my feet and hurrying towards the lapping waves before any of the cocky surfer boys fancied a bit of pointing and sniggering *my* way.

Actually, I was glad to have a second on my own, to think a slightly mad thought. It's just that the fur on my leg... It wasn't just silly, it was a *clue*.

Call me insane (and my friends might have, if they'd known what was on my mind), but ever since Peaches had strolled into my room and adopted me as his owner, he'd had a habit of leaving signs for me every time something or someone important was about to lurch into my life.

It had happened with Joseph's house, it had happened with TJ, Rachel, Megan and Amber. So what was this latest sign trying to tell me? Was it something to do with the surfer boys? Tilda Gilmore, maybe? Or that bizarre message up on the lamp-post?

As I stood deep in thought in the shallows, letting the waves lap my legs back to normal, I found my gaze held by a swirl of seagulls flapping and darting directly above my head.

Then I realized that there's nothing guaranteed to put you off your deep, mystical thoughts quicker than the prospect of getting pooped on by a seagull – or run over by a surfboard – and scuttled back up the beach pronto...

Chapter 3

A visitor of the unexpected kind

Dad was talking. I was listening, but not really understanding.

"That's the trouble with mortar and lath," he muttered, scratching his blond, dust-speckled hair. "It's so old, it just crumbles. So that's why I'll have to go for the plasterboard and light skim option..."

OK, looking round my building-site of a bedroom, I guessed that DIY gibberish translated as: "I know it looks terrible but I'll fix it."

It's funny, back in London, Dad used to go to work in flashy suits, listening to his headphones and reading magazines about the latest technological gizmos. But since we'd moved to Portbay and my parents' "dream cottage" (i.e. dump with potential), Dad had tried to reinvent himself as one of those blokes off those TV programmes where they transform someone's cruddy flat into a stately home with en-suite helicopter landing pad on a budget of £12.50, all in the space of half an hour.

Unluckily for this house, our family, and in particular, my bedroom, Dad was "learning as he went along", which meant most of the house was a mix of original bits like the fireplaces (nice), new bits that Dad had fixed (fine), and odd bits that Dad had started/not finished/ messed up (nasty). Mum had come up with clever ways to disguise the nasty stuff till Dad got around to sorting it: she threw rugs and pretty material over the worst offenders, or stuck big vases of flowers in the way to brighten the place up. But some things she couldn't do anything about ... like Dad getting in a muddle with the plumbing and fixing the toilet cistern up to the hot water pipe. (Having a blast of steam on your bottom when you were having a wee was very, *very* odd.)

"How long will it take, Dad?" I asked, hoping I didn't sound ungrateful and impatient.

It was an important question – from tonight I was going to have to sleep on a blow-up bed on the floor of the twins' room, which was going to be zero fun, unless drifting off to sleep in a room that whiffs of milk and wet nappies and being woken by two bouncy toddlers at quarter to dawn in the morning is your idea of fun.

"Let's see..." Dad ummed, going silent for a

minute as he calculated how many aeons it would take to make my room habitable. (*Please don't make me have to sleep in the boys' room till I'm eighteen*, I thought to myself.)

While Dad ummed and pulled funny thinking faces to himself, I stared out of the open window and into the garden – at the little outhouse that was my den, specifically. Once I'd had this chat with Dad, I wanted to tiptoe down the stairs – avoiding Jake and Jamie who were lobbing Lego at each other while Mum was on the phone last time I looked – and get out there. On the way back from the beach just now, I'd been thinking about getting my art stuff out and coming up with a new look for the ninja fairies I liked to doodle. It'd still be pretty, and funky, and sort of manga, but I wanted to try a new twist … a *Tilda* twist. A fairy with a sharp black bob, tutu and stripy tights – how cool would that be?

Almost as cool as Peaches hopping his hefty self up on to the bedroom window sill at that very second and giving me the catty equivalent of a knowing smile…

"Well, let's see, Stella," Dad started up, just as I was thinking that Tilda might be the focus of Peaches' spook clues. "It's Sunday today, so I should get this all back to bare brick by—"

A thundering of four two-year-old feet on the stairs stopped Dad in his tracks.

"Jake! Jamie! I said *stop*!!" we both heard Mum yell, as she thundered up after them.

"Uh-oh – I should've fixed up that stair-gate like I promised," Dad muttered, looking round in a panic.

Dad was looking around in a panic because...

a) the twins were dangerous enough around a pot of yoghurt and some clothes pegs (one gas hob hadn't worked too well since Jake poured strawberry Onken on it, and Jamie had red pinch marks all over his legs for two days after he pegged himself). How lethal would they be if they got their hands on Dad's sledgehammer and drill? And...

b) there wasn't a door to close, as Dad had taken every door inside the house off and sent them away to be stripped (well, they were stacked round the side of the house, *waiting* to be stripped, and currently gathering a fine collection of cobwebs).

"Gotcha!" I yelped, catching one tornado of a boy as he hurtled into the room. Mum, coming up at the rear, neatly scooped up the second tornado before either of them could do any damage.

"TOYS! Jamie wanna PLAY!!" Jamie shrieked

and wriggled in my arms, pointing to a nail-gun on the floor.

"NOT toys!" Mum said sharply to him, before turning her gaze on me. "Hey, guess who was on the phone just now, Stella?"

I ran through the obvious people in my head: Auntie V, or Mum's friends from London; maybe Granny or Grandad Stansfield in Norfolk. But before I got the chance to suggest any of them, Mum said: "Mrs Samson!"

Er, I didn't know a Mrs Samson. Did I? Was she some old teacher of mine from primary school? Or some long-time-ago neighbour and chum of Granny Jones, getting in touch for a catch-up and a reminisce?

"Megan's mum!" my own mum prompted me.

Of course! Megan's last name was Samson... As for Mrs Samson, the last I'd seen of her and Megan's dad had been when they were angrily bundling their daughters into the back of their car, suspecting them both (and me, TJ and Rachel) of mega-bad behaviour. Since they'd got back home, I knew from Megan that her mum and dad now had the true story; i.e. Megan's older sister Naomi had been busy blaming all of *us* just to cover up her secret holiday romance with Si Riley and their *joint* mega-bad behaviour...

"*Megan's* mum?" I blurted out now. "How come?"

Was she phoning to say something had happened to Megan? It couldn't have – Megan had only texted me an hour ago, asking for my home phone number. But then she hadn't got back to me when I'd asked her why...

"Jake, *stop* it! We'll play outside in a minute!" said Mum, distracted from our conversation for a second by a small boy grabbing her nose and twisting it. "She phoned to ask a favour, Stella. Megan's parents have to go away to a funeral at the weekend; I think their oldest daughter is staying with a friend, but everyone they know locally who could look after Megan is on holiday. So Megan suggested coming here."

"They want Megan to come stay with *us* this weekend?!" I said excitedly.

Yay for visitors of the unexpected kind – specially when they happened to be Megan.

"Well, I wouldn't say her parents *wanted* her to," Mum said wryly, trying to hold Jake on her hip as he started to climb up her chest. "I think they're just desperate. And I mean I understand their concern – you and Megan were only holiday friends, after all. But we had a long chat, and I think I managed to reassure her that we're decent

36

people who aren't into cannibalism or witchcraft or whatever."

"You got a bit of a cross-examination, then?" Dad smiled at Mum's words.

"Something like that." Mum laughed. "I didn't dare tell her that her daughter's probably going to have to sleep on a lilo in the hall though!"

"Where *is* Megan going to sleep? And when's she coming? How's she getting here?" I asked, questions and complications rattling around my head.

"Her folks are going to put her on a train on Friday morning, and we'll meet her at the train station here," Mum reassured me on a couple of points.

"Friday? I'll easily have your room done by then! It'll even be decorated!" said Dad, trying to reassure me on another point. (I *wanted* to believe him, but the throws and vases of flowers round our house kind of made that a tough call...)

"WANNA CUDDLE CAT!!!" Jamie suddenly shrieked in my ear, and slithered down out of my arms like he was an eel covered in margarine.

As he bolted towards the window, Peaches elegantly plopped off the sill, on to the kitchen roof below, safely out of reach of any unwanted, vice-like hugs.

"WANNA CLIMB!!"

"Nope," I said firmly, quickly following Jamie and lassoing him with my arms as he kneed his way up on to the window sill.

Down below in the garden, Peaches' red fur glinted as he slunk along, like a flurry of flames through the long grass.

As if he knew I was looking at him (actually, there was no question – I was and he did), Peaches turned and gave me a green-eyed wink.

"Watch out for more clues..." he might as well have purred out loud.

Before I could think any more about whether my cat was seriously psychic (or I was seriously going nuts to think that), reality hit.

Actually, reality *bit*.

"Jamie! NO! Let *go* of your sister!" said Dad, as Jamie did an excellent Rottweiler impersonation and dug his baby teeth in even deeper...

Chapter 4

Good news and, um, not so good news. . .

Rachel narrowed her dark, Siamesey eyes and gently ran her finger round the indentations that Jamie's teeth had left yesterday.

"Looks a bit like the swirly Celtic circle tattoo my brother Si keeps threatening to get," she murmured.

"*Please* tell me he wants to get the tattoo on his arm, and not his cheek," I muttered back.

Having a large, round, bruise-like bite mark on your face is *so* not a good look. It's not as if you can dab some concealer on it or stick a plaster over it. Maybe if I'd been Rachel I could've brushed a curtain of long, sleek brown hair over the right-hand side of my face in a very dramatic stylee. But I'm Stella, with goldy-brown tight curls that are into sproinging around rather than draping dramatically.

"What did your mum and dad say about it?" asked Rachel, still staring.

Someone else was staring too, I noticed – a middle-aged journalist, peering over his desk partition and probably wondering what two thirteen-year-old girls were doing hovering around the offices of the *Portbay Journal* on a Monday morning.

"They told Jamie off, but then they said to me that it's just a phase lots of toddlers go through."

"Yeah, either that, or he's a trainee vampire," Rachel suggested.

I was about to laugh when she suggested something far worse.

"Did you see the way that reporter girl checked it out and grinned? Bet you ten pounds she thought it was some weird kind of love-bite..."

Urgh ... the middle-aged journalist bloke probably thought the same. I bet he was staring over right now thinking how he'd write a feature about the youth of Portbay running wild and getting up to all sorts. I was just on the verge of dying of shame and crawling on my hands and knees out of the office when Jane Williams – the reporter who'd interviewed me and my friends about Joseph's house and got the whole saving-the-chandelier ball rolling – bounded back over.

"There you go! All scanned in, Stella," she said brightly, handing me back the framed photo that had languished in the kitchen of the Shingle café for so long, until Amber asked Phil the owner if I could have it.

"And now we know the surname Joseph was using, I've got a junior reporter on the case," Jane continued, leaning over her desk and scooping up a tape recorder and sunglasses, ready for her next job.

"On the case?" I repeated, slapping my hand over my cheek and hoping it looked to her like I was striking an interested pose, rather than just covering up a weird love bite.

"Well, since you found that dedication on the bench in Pavilion Park, we know for sure that Joseph adopted the surname of the Grainger family, right?" said Jane.

"Right." I nodded. The dedication and photo were the reasons I'd dropped by the newspaper office this morning (taking Rachel along for company and courage, since strolling into newspaper offices isn't exactly something I make a habit of).

"So now our junior reporter can start trawling though local records of births, marriages and deaths, and see if we can find out more about what Joseph did with his life after he left the old house and went out into the world."

And where he'd gone in the world couldn't have been *too* far away.

For a start, the photo seemed to be local-ish. Jane had been pretty excited about the grainy old black-and-white framed snap. It showed an older Joseph, standing proudly beside a bride, who we'd figured out had to be his daughter. Jane was sure that once they'd printed it in the paper, someone would recognize the church they were standing in front of.

And then there was the fact that he'd sat in that spot in Pavilion Park often enough for his granddaughter to think of putting up a dedication in his name on the bench.

"OK, girls, sorry to rush you but I'd better get going – got some surfers to interview…"

Oh, *them*. If those lads were already big-headed enough to act like they owned the beach and could snigger openly at people on it, how big-headed were they all going to be knowing there was going to be a story about them in the local paper?

"Stella…" muttered Rachel, suddenly nudging me. "The money – remember?"

"Oh, yeah!" I said, whipping my hand away from my face and rifling in my pocket for the fifty pounds Rachel's mum had given me for the fairy pictures she'd sold in her shop. "I wanted to give this to the Sponsor a Crystal campaign…"

"There's no need," said a deep voice, which happened to belong to the middle-aged journalist bloke, who'd left his desk and partition behind and strolled over to join us.

What's his problem? I fretted. Wouldn't he let wild child thirteen-year-olds with love bites on their cheeks donate money to a good cause?

"Of course!" Jane suddenly said. "I forgot to tell you – the museum says they've raised enough money in the last few days to get the chandelier moved – we've got the story in the paper today."

"Here's a print-out of what we're running," said the bloke, handing me a sheet to read. "Once the chandelier's in situ, we'll have to get you and your friends along to the museum for a follow-up."

I wasn't really sure what "in situ" meant, and he was using a lot of what I supposed was fancy journalist jargon, but I wasn't really listening – my eyes were too busy skimming the article.

"What's *that* bit about?" Rachel suddenly said, pointing to some thick black lettering under a photo of Joseph's house. "It says the house is getting demolished next week!"

"But that's not right!" I burst out. "It's not getting knocked down for a while yet!"

"The council changed the date – they brought it forward," said Jane matter-of-factly, as she zipped up her bag. "Which makes it all the better that the museum got the money for the chandelier together so quickly."

I thought I'd got my head around the old place getting flattened, but from the wave of shock I felt rippling from my tummy to my head and back again, I obviously hadn't. When I'd stumbled upon Joseph's house, that first week I'd been in Portbay, it had felt like coming across the most awesome, nail-bitingly spooky secret in the world. I just couldn't imagine it not sitting grandly in the middle of Sugar Bay any more.

Worse than that, I felt a sharp stab of hurt in my throat as I imagined the bulldozers and the wrecking crews hacking its walls to pieces, tearing the memories (and ghosts?) of the place apart...

I *guess* Jane and the other journalist bloke said bye to us, and I *guess* we said bye to them, but it all happened in a bit of a haze. The next thing I knew was that me and Rachel were walking along the pavement on the high street, the scent of saltwater on the breeze helping to tingle my senses back to normal, even though I still felt like I had a heavy brick lodged in my stomach.

"There's never been anything in Sugar Bay

except Joseph's house," said Rachel. "Before it was built, it was just sand and sea and seagulls and cliffs, I guess. It's weird thinking that by this time next summer, it'll be full of posh chalets and holidaymakers…"

I was so lost in that depressing thought that I almost missed seeing the A4 sheet of paper. Luckily, my feet were paying more attention and stopped dead on the corner of the High Street and the alley that led to The Vault.

"Look – it's one of those messages again!" I said, pointing to the taped-to-the-bricks sheet with the squiggled-on writing.

For a small town that looked a bit corny and dull from the outside, Portbay was jam-packed with freakiness.

Who knew I'd find Joseph's house?

Who knew I'd find out that the little girl who'd grown up there would turn out to have lived in *my* house as an old lady?

Who knew a spooky fat cat would adopt me as its owner?

Who knew that spooky fat cat would point me in the direction of all the new friends I had?

And that's not even *starting* on stuff like mad-round-the-edges Mrs Sticky Toffee who I kept bumping into. Or the psycho seagull who used to stalk TJ. Or the tap-dancing librarian. Or the bunch of goosebumpy coincidences that kept happening around me.

These squiggly messages were just some more freakiness that I was sure would eventually unravel.

"Stella! What are you doing?" gasped Rachel, as I pulled the paper of the wall, folded it and stuck it in my pocket.

"Well, does it say 'Private Property' on it?" I asked her.

"Maybe." Rachel shrugged. "We don't know *what* it says."

"Yeah, well it's just as likely to say 'Please take me home and translate me'."

And that's exactly what I was going to try and do.

At least, I was going to waft it under someone's gingery whiskers and see what his Fat Furry Spookiness made of it...

Chapter 5

The thing about Tilda

"When men are together, it's like they're having a *loudness* competition," I remember my very chic Auntie V once saying dryly, when her, me and Mum were hunting for a café after shopping at Camden Market one Saturday, and happened to pass an open-doored pub where tons of guys were hollering at the footie on a big screen.

And it was true now too; at the back of the café, three surfer lads were bellowing with laughter, while a third one pulled a stupid, sour face and wore part of his black wetsuit draped across his head. What was *that* about?

I didn't have much time to think, 'cause Rachel had started muttering something.

"*'Someone my dad used to work with – I've never met him,'*" she said, reading aloud a text that had just flashed on to the screen of her mobile.

"What's that?" I asked her.

"I just wrote '*Why are you coming? Who died?*' to Megan," Rachel answered, unaware or unconcerned about how horribly tactless her question could've been.

"Lift, please!" Phil the café owner suddenly ordered.

Rachel grabbed her mobile, TJ lifted his music magazine, and I made a grab for the folded-out A4 sheet we'd all been poring over.

Flappity-FLOOF!!

The new plastic-coated tablecloth sailed out and flopped down on to our table. It had a pattern of red peppers, green peppers and sunflowers dotted all over it.

"Great! That's the last one," Phil muttered happily to himself, ambling off just as Amber ambled over, with TJ's lunch on a tray.

"Ouch! Does that hurt, Stella?"

TJ's burger nearly slipped off its plate as Amber caught sight of my cheek.

"I got bitten. By a rabid twin," I said with a shrug. "It's an occupational hazard of being an older sister of little monsters."

"Maybe your parents could put him in quarantine till he's old enough to grow out of the biting stage!" Amber suggested with a smile.

"You know something? It *stinks* in here!"

That was Rachel. Grumbling. And wrinkling her nose.

"It's just chips! How can you say chips stink?" said TJ, looking down at the plate of golden brown chips (and burger) that Amber had just placed in front of him.

"It's chips and *paint*," I pointed out, looking around at the newly sunshine-yellowed walls of the seafront café. Living in a house that was a permanent DIY project, I was well used to the strangely mixed scents of food and paint. In fact, a lasagne without the whiff of Dulux wouldn't seem right to me any more.

"He was up all night painting the place," Amber explained, nodding at Phil, who was now standing at the gurgling coffee machine, looking like he might fall asleep where he was and end up with a nose covered in cappuccino froth.

It was Monday lunchtime, and me and Rachel had come straight from the newspaper office to the café to meet TJ. The three of us were sitting at the window seat, with its great view of the sea – and two blokes' legs.

The legs were on ladders, and the two blokes were carefully fixing up a sign with the words "Hot Pepper Jelly Café" spelt out in large, bright, orange and red Mexican-style writing. Watching transfixed on the pavement were TJ's little sister Ellie, who was "sharing" her lunch with Bob the dog (i.e. while Ellie wasn't looking, Bob bit off a corner of her cheese and pickle sandwich). The hair on Bob's face was pinned back with a cute pair of Hello Kitty hairslides, I noticed. Apparently Ellie had seen him in the pink spangly grips yesterday and decided to style him that way from now on. Poor Bob...

But enough of doggy makeovers: the makeover of the café had started last week, after I (accidentally) helped nearly set fire to the place. (It's a long story, involving an overweight seagull, a doughnut and a neon shop sign. Don't ask.)

Luckily for me, even though he hadn't actually *planned* on a makeover, Phil seemed to be really enjoying transforming the dull-ish Shingle café into something brighter and funkier. As well as painting the white walls yellow, and shelling out for new tablecloths, he'd had new menus printed (with the same funky lettering and a cartoony red chilli pepper icon on it) and serviettes to match. He'd taken down all the framed black-and-white photos of old-time Portbay too, to be replaced with posters of fiery peppers and juicy tomatos, all in close-up and mega-tastic detail.

Some of the old lady customers were looking a bit confused and bemused by the change of scenery. But anyone under the age of seventy seemed to be smiling and nodding as they gawped around. Rachel's brother Si and his mates approved of it too, I was pretty sure. They were all hunkered around the big table at the back, and their goth-meets-grunge looks fitted in a whole lot better with the full-on colours than the previous pastels, gingham tablecloths and corny fake flowers in vases.

Tilda Gilmore was with them, as usual, but her normally sulky expression was temporarily replaced with a glimmer of interest as she glanced around at the revamped walls. She was even running one hand – in a black, lacy, fingerless glove – across a poster beside her as Si and co lazily chatted.

And then it dawned on me ... the surfer pulling the sour face, with his wetsuit dolloped on his head – he was imitating Tilda. They were laughing at her *again*. What were they *like*?

"Are you on a break soon?" I became aware of TJ asking Amber.

I turned my attention back to my friends, and noticed that Amber had put very cute tiny plaits in the front of her hair, to keep it back from her face. She was wearing a tiny bit of brown mascara, which made her hazel eyes seem huge.

"In about another ten minutes," she said, checking her watch. "Oops!"

Amber might not look so much like the glum, shy waitress she was until recently, but she was still as *useless* a waitress as ever. Checking your watch while you're holding a glass of Coke and ice isn't *really* a great idea.

"I'll get a mop for that…" she mumbled, staring at the puddle of Coke before heading off.

"Hey – we haven't told Amber that Megan's coming!" said TJ, taking a bite of his burger.

While we'd been waiting for our order, I'd filled him in with tales of the Sponsor a Crystal campaign, demolition squads, Megan's visit at the weekend and more strange squiggled messages popping up.

"Hey, doughball," Rachel sighed in TJ's direction, "Amber's *hardly* going to be excited, is she? In case you've forgotten, we were mates with Megan *before* we were mates with Amber. They don't even know each other!"

"Oh, yeah!" TJ nodded, taking absolutely no offence at Rachel's sarky tone.

"Hope they get on…" I said, though I couldn't see how goofy-and-nice Megan and shy-and-nice Amber *wouldn't* get on, really.

"So what will we do while Megan's here?" asked TJ.

"Well, if the surfers are still around, we can go and look at them…"

"Great," grumbled TJ, pulling a just-kill-me-now face.

As for me, well, I wasn't too keen on the idea either. But it did get me glancing out of the window – scanning the waves. Not that I could see much sea – there was too much blocking my view: the guys fixing up the sign, Bob and Ellie, traffic cruising the promenade, and holidaymakers bumbling along in the sunshine. I even caught a glimpse of green and pink over by the railings; Mrs Sticky Toffee, in her apple-coloured raincoat and candyfloss hat. She was probably rifling in her tiny handbag for sweet treats to feed the psycho seagull.

I might not have been able to spy a surfer, but at least all the staring into space seemed to let a thought zap into my head.

"*I* know! Dad says my room will be finished by Friday – why don't we have a girly sleepover to celebrate?"

"'Cause your room'll probably still smell of paint?" said Rachel.

"Stop moaning! It'll be fun!" I laughed at her.

"Yeah, fun – if you're a *girl*!" grumbled TJ, obviously feeling mightily left out.

My mind was faffing around, trying to quickly think of ways to console him, when I noticed a flush-faced Amber, hurrying over to our table, a mop in her hand. She looked like she might cry. She looked as if someone had popped the bubble of confidence she'd finally developed these last few days.

"What's up?" I asked, as she threw herself tight-lipped into her mopping.

"*Tilda's* what's up," she muttered. "I was just on my way back here to clean up when Si called me over."

"What did he want?"

Rachel had more-or-less blackmailed her brother into being Amber's last date on Saturday at the dreaded family wedding. But I think it still freaked her out a bit that Amber and Si had got on so well.

"It was no big wow. He was only talking to me about a *Twilight* DVD he'd promised to lend me," said Amber, shrugging her shoulders. "And then Tilda barks at me that her order is late, and I said sorry … and then she said I *should* be, and I'd better sort it out or she'd tell Phil."

"That's pretty rude!" Rachel sympathized, which was pretty funny, since she was quite good at being rude herself.

"Yeah but the worst thing is, I didn't even *take* her order – it was one of the other girls. What makes her think she can talk to me like that!"

My sympathy for Tilda – for the mickey-taking going on that she wasn't even aware of – vanished like a puff of gurgling coffee machine steam.

I gazed towards the table at the back of the café, where Si Riley was now lost in some yakkings with his blokey mates. Tilda wasn't joining in; she was just sitting staring at Si, her kohl-rimmed eyes blinking fast, flashing glimpses of the dark, pearly, greeny-blue shadow smoothed across her eyelids. Greeny-blue, like those two darting, dancing dragonflies in my garden a couple of days ago.

And then I got it: what made Tilda talk to Amber that way, I mean.

The thing about Tilda was … as obvious to me at that minute as being sure that Bob was a dog and my cat smelled (strangely) of peaches and cream.

Oh, yes, the thing about Tilda was, she had a crush the size of Portbay on her best boy mate, Si Riley…

Chapter 6

A 100% not sure. . .

It was Amber's break.

And as the surfers surfed (like they owned the beach), and the seagulls swooped (like they wanted their waves to themselves again), three girls (three and a *half*, if you counted five-year-old Ellie), one boy and a daft dog hunkered down on the sands, licking ice lollies and musing over my suspicions about Tilda.

Actually, they were more than just suspicions. Since I'd seen Tilda glowering at Amber back in the café, I'd suddenly had a clear memory of the way Tilda had glowered at Megan's sister when Naomi was having her holiday romance with Si. Of *course* Tilda was nuts about him, and of *course* she was going to glower at anyone she suspected of taking his attention away from her.

"Tilda fancying Si..." muttered TJ, holding one ice lolly for himself, and another for Bob to lick. "Well, *that's* a turn-up."

"Yeah, but so what? No *way* is anything going to happen between my brother and Tilda."

Rachel shook her head, her hair falling back into place sheeny-shinily, shampoo-ad style.

"But why not? Tilda's pretty, in an interesting way. And I know she dresses kind of mad, but it's not like Si and the others are into smart shirts and sensible trousers!" I said, thinking of Si's pierced lip and purple-tinged black hair, and his mates' rock T-shirts and flapping, trailing baggy jeans.

"There's no *way*, 'cause I know for a fact that my brother only sees her as a friend; like just another one of the lads."

"Yeah, a lad in a *tutu*..." TJ sniggered.

"Whatever," said Rachel, shrugging off TJ's quip.

"But if they're friends already, doesn't that already mean he likes her in a way?" I suggested, not really sure how people got together, since I wasn't the world's greatest expert.

"But that's like saying you and TJ are friends, so why don't *you* two go out!" said Rachel, much to my shame. (Instant images of the Emergency Kiss boinged into my head.)

"Yeah, right!" I said, laughing a little too hard and hoping no one would notice how suddenly pink I was feeling. Especially TJ. Luckily, they all started laughing too. And luckily, Rachel decided to change the subject and give me a hard time instead. Which, trust me, was a *lot* easier to handle.

"Why are you sticking up for Tilda anyway, Stella? She was horrible to Amber in the café just now!"

I scrunched up my nose, as if to say, "I dunno". But I *did* know.

"Unrequited love" ... it sounds like such a romantic phrase, doesn't it? But it's not romantic at all, that crushing, soul-sucking feeling of being crazy about someone when they're not in the *slightest* bit crazy about you back.

Five weeks. That's how long Frankie (my best mate back in London) and Seb (the boy I'd been crazy about back in London) had been going out now. And while it still felt bizarre, it didn't hurt-to-the-core like it once did.

Spotting that aura of one-way love seeping off Tilda, I wished I knew her well enough to be able to say, "It's not going to happen between you two, but it won't feel so bad, eventually ... honest!"

And I wasn't the only one feeling sorry for her.

"I wish I was brave enough to go and tell her that I'm only friends with Si," murmured Amber. "But if I did, then she'd know I'd figured out that she fancied him, and that would probably make her feel ten times worse!"

Rachel frowned at Amber and then me, as if she couldn't quite believe that *both* of us had let Tilda and her bad behaviour off the hook.

"Her room's painted *black*, y'know."

I didn't really understand what Rachel meant by that. That Si couldn't possibly fancy Tilda because her walls were the colour of binbags?

"*And* she's supposed to have a pet rat!" TJ chipped in gleefully.

I mean, yeah, so black wasn't the sort of shade I'd be asking Dad to paint my room later on in the week, and I didn't see myself swapping Peaches for a rat to cuddle any time soon, but why would that sort of stuff put Si Riley off? He wasn't exactly a rose-patterns and fluffy bunny kind of guy.

And hold on … when I'd first got to know him, TJ told me he was treated like an outsider by people at school because of his height (or lack of it). And Rachel went from being Miss Popular to Miss Nobody after her seizures scared her horrible friends away. So it bugged me a bit – the way Rachel and TJ weren't just telling me interesting facts about Tilda, but were saying it in that sort of gossipy, "isn't-that-nuts?" way. Y'know – like anyone who wasn't snoringly normal must be a total outcast.

Wait a sec – Amber was in Tilda's year at school. And Amber was used to being an outsider too. Maybe she'd have a different take on her…?

"Is Tilda in any of your classes?" I asked her.

"Nope," said Amber, staring down at the A4 sheet of gobbledegook I'd let her have a look at. "I don't really know her except to look at. But I heard a couple of people say that she's into black magic."

"How do they know that?" I frowned, wondering if Tilda had put a hex on a teacher and made him burp the entire lesson or something.

"Apparently, someone said she went to Cornwall on holiday last year and went to a witchcraft museum!" Amber replied.

The witchcraft museum in Boscastle … my London friend Lauren went there once with her family, I remembered. *Having a great time*, she'd written on a postcard. *Been to a monkey sanctuary, a witchcraft museum, the Eden Project and eaten so many scones and cream I feel sick.* Going to the witchcraft museum hadn't exactly turned Lauren to the dark side, any more than going to the monkey sanctuary had turned her into a long-tailed woolly monkey.

"Yes," I frowned, "but that hardly makes Tilda a goth version of Hermione from Harry Potter, does—"

"It's in code, that's for sure…" Amber suddenly mumbled an interruption, her finger trailing along a line of scribbled unknowns. "Me and my dad used to muck around writing stuff in code to each other when I was younger."

"Did you? What kind of stuff?" TJ asked animatedly.

"Like writing words backwards. F'r instance, 'Ym-eman-si-rebma'!"

"What?" I squeaked, along with Rachel and TJ.

"Ym-eman-si-rebma…" repeated Amber, going a bit pink-cheeked as we all stared at her in confusion.

"And ym-eman-si-eille!" a small, clear voice piped up, giggling.

This time, me, TJ and Rachel all turned and stared in confusion at Ellie.

"It's easy!" She laughed. "Amber said 'my name is Amber', and I said 'my name is Ellie' – only we did it with the words all tangly-up and back-to-front!"

Great. A five-year-old kid was smarter than a whole bunch of us thirteen year olds put together.

"Can I take this home, Stella?" asked Amber, pointing to the "message". "'Cause maybe Dad and I can figure out what it's supposed to be."

I *had* planned to waft the paper under Peaches'

nose, but then even if he *did* know what it meant, I wouldn't be able to understand, since I didn't speak cat-ish, and he didn't speak English (probably).

"Yeah, sure." I nodded at Amber. "But this is more complicated than just stuff written backwards, isn't it?"

"It's a kind of aflabet!" said Ellie, leaning over for a closer look and dribbling strawberry Mini Milk on the squiggles.

Even though Ellie couldn't *pronounce* the word alphabet properly, I was tempted to hand the message over to her and see what she made of it. Maybe her lightning, five-year-old mind would figure out its secret message, and who had written it, whether it was aliens, practical jokers or –

"Tilda!" I muttered, interrupting myself.

"What about her?" asked Rachel, following my gaze.

"Look – she's just come out of the café, and it looks like she's going into Madame Xara's!"

Tilda was poised at the door of the clairvoyant's shop, her finger on the doorbell.

"Maybe Tilda is a trainee witch or something!" exclaimed Amber, turning round to stare too. "Maybe she's going for psychic lessons with Madame Xara!"

I couldn't see that happening. Madame Xara the clairvoyant did a roaring trade with holidaymakers, who didn't know her reputation well enough to realize she was rubbish. Her psychic powers only extended to telling people non-thrilling stuff like the fact that they'd probably get their hair cut soon, or go on holiday sometime (pretty accurate if she was talking to holidaymakers, I guess). She also worked part-time in the cheese shop, which didn't seem particularly psychic to me. ("Would you like your palm read, along with that slab of cheddar? Hmm?")

"Maybe Tilda's desperate. Maybe she's going to ask Madame Xara to look into her future and see if Si will ever fall for her," I said, feeling a) really sorry for Tilda, and b) sure as sure could be that Tilda was no trainee witch.

Er...

You know what I was saying about b)?

Well, maybe I wasn't a *hundred* percent sure about that after all. 'Cause just as Madame Xara's door opened and she was ushered in, Tilda paused and turned sharply, her dragonfly eyes suddenly locking on to mine from across the promenade...

Chapter 7

Zillion-mile-an-hour scaredy legs

Guess which one of these statements is true:

a) I'd woken up this Tuesday morning feeling absolutely fantastic, after a great night's sleep, filled with lovely dreams.

b) I'd woken up this Tuesday morning feeling pants, after a rotten night's sleep, filled with snoring and missiles.

The answer – drum roll please – is b).

The snoring came from two matching small boys (when one stopped, the other would start). I'd stayed awake most of the night, and had been tempted at one point to text Megan to pass the time, or even drag my blow-up bed downstairs to the living room. But I'd worried that the bleeping of the keypad or the squelch of the airbed would wake the boys and start a duet of wailing.

Anyway, I'd finally fallen asleep, *just* as a bunch of over-excited birds starting tweetering at the dawn outside my brothers' bedroom window.

And that's when the missiles started.

The missiles were aimed by Jake and Jamie, who'd ping-ed wide awake at five a.m. and – thrilled to see me lying on their floor – decided to use me as target practice.

The Fimble, the teddy and the soggy nappy didn't hurt at all, but I was sure the plastic cup had left a dent in my head. As for the Noddy book … well, now I had a memento of *both* my brothers on my face – a paper cut on my lip from the book Jake chucked, and the slowing fading bite mark from Jamie on my cheek.

And now, five hours later, in the crowded hallway of the museum, a grey-haired woman narrowed her eyes suspiciously at me and clutched her handbag a little tighter. No wonder – thanks to my face I looked like I'd been in a street fight with a pit bull. I bet the woman was wondering why a teenage delinquent wanted to hang out in the local museum. Bet she thought I was here to scribble rude graffiti on the Roman vases or something.

I tried to smile reassuringly at her, but immediately winced as the cut on my lip opened again. Great – it was bleeding. Now the woman would think I was a teenage delinquent vampire who'd had a street fight with a pit bull, and drunk its blood.

Little did she know, I was a well-brought-up, responsible citizen of Portbay. I was even about to donate a box of historical bits and bobs to the museum.

Still, it was going to be tough to attract the museum assistant's attention, and at the moment there seemed to be no way to get over to the desk so I could put my precious cargo down. The whole of the reception area of the museum was squashed full of a coach-trip's worth of grey-and-white-haired elderly women, all of them on a mission to buy postcards or tea towels with images of old Portbay printed on them.

I shifted the box around nervously (being scowled at *does* have a habit of making you nervous), still feeling the scowling woman's eyes boring into me. If I'd been a bit cheeky (a *lot* cheeky) like my friend Frankie back in London, I'd have stuck my tongue out at her by now.

Hmm… Maybe that's what I should do! Forget about being a well-brought-up, model citizen for a second and stick my tongue out at this rudely staring person!

Deciding I should act quickly before I chickened out, I turned sharply to her … and then noticed she was slightly cross-eyed or something. I mean, it was obvious that she was trying to focus on me, but her scowl was shooting straight over my shoulder.

Er … she *was* scowling at *me*, wasn't she?

I swivelled around to see Tilda Gilmore, decked out in her tutu, leather jacket and stripy tights.

OK, so the woman *wasn't* scowling at me, and *didn't* have a squint. (Just as well I hadn't let my tongue loose.)

As for Tilda, she was too busy to notice that she was the subject of any disapproving looks – she was staring at the framed oil painting of Joseph hanging on the wall. Or at least, she was looking at something beside it.

The painting I knew pretty well – it had been part of a recent bequest to the museum, and I'd got a sneak preview of it from the curator, before it had gone on show. But I needed to get closer to see what exactly had caught Tilda's eye.

I started to shuffle up beside her casually, even though it's hard to look casual when you're carrying an awkward cardboard box.

And when I was close enough, I saw that she was reading *my* story (well, *our* story). There was the newspaper cutting – under perspex – with me and TJ and everyone, standing in the old dilapidated ballroom of the house in Sugar Bay.

"I didn't know you'd started everyone getting

so interested in Joseph and the big house," Tilda startled me by saying, without even turning around.

Gulp. Maybe she is *just a tiny little bit of a witch!* whispered the right-hand, more whimsical side of my brain (i.e. the side that was sure Peaches had special powers).

Or maybe she'd spotted you already, and the rustle of all the newspaper padding in the box gave you away! argued the sensible, left-hand side of my brain (i.e. the side that was convinced Peaches was an ordinary, fat, scruffy cat).

"I saw you come in a second ago," she explained, pleasing the left-hand side of my brain very much.

As she spoke, Tilda moved her head to face me, and I got the full-on effect – dainty doll's features framed by deep-black bob, and masked in dramatic make-up: dark red lips, black-rimmed eyes and that shimmering dragonfly greeny-blue on her eyelids. I suddenly had a yearning to get a glimpse of her parents – they had to be pretty laid-back and funky themselves to let a fifteen year old dress the way Tilda did, never mind paint her room black and have a pet rat…

"Yeah. I – I mean, we all really love Joseph's house, and just wanted to do something to help,"

I stumbled out, in answer to what she'd said initially.

"That's brilliant. The old house is just great – I love going over there on my own, and just drifting through those amazing old rooms," said Tilda wistfully, putting a purple-painted, bitten nail up against the newspaper story. "Until they boarded it up, course."

I'd never seen Tilda there. You never saw *anyone* there. It felt strange knowing she'd walked around the same, secret rooms and corridors as I had, and probably got her clothes stuck on the same, tangly, overgrown bushes in the garden as me.

"Great painting, isn't it?" I said, because I didn't know what else to say to this pretty, pretty-weird girl.

"Mmm," she nodded, staring at Joseph as a young man wearing a thick leather apron. "I got a real shock when I saw it here, 'cause I was only a little kid the last time."

"The last time?"

"The last time I saw it, I mean. We used to live next door to Miss Duggan –"

Tilda tapped a purple-nailed finger on a brass plaque that read, *Kindly bequeathed by Mary Duggan.*

"– and it's always stuck in my mind."

My heart went scrunch for a second time. It was like I was permanently on the lookout for clues; a detective on the trail of anything to do with Joseph or Elize Grainger or the house. Inside the cardboard box I was carrying were the clues I'd come across so far: a watercolour fairy painted by Elize as an old lady, a rusty old box of paints, a chipped cup with roses painted on it, a small wooden box with the initials *E.G.* neatly carved on the top (empty, except for a discoloured gold-ish metal button, which used to be on the uniform Joseph wore when he was the family's servant boy). There was also a brown felt hat with ribbons and a yellowed newspaper dated 1930, with a story about Elize Grainger, who was celebrating her hundredth birthday – in what was now our garden.

And now this could be *another* part of the puzzle.

"Was Mary Duggan a relative of Joseph's?" I asked, my heart pitter-pattering with excitement.

"I don't think so," said Tilda, shaking her head at the same time as she shook away any hopes I had of solving the puzzle. "I think she just collected antiques and interesting old stuff. Anyway, she wasn't black, like Joseph."

Even if this Miss Duggan had been white as a snowball in a snowstorm, I knew more than most that this might not completely rule out the fact that she and Joseph were related somewhere along the way.

"My grandfather was black," I told Tilda. "He was from Barbados –"

"– same as Joseph!" she said at the same time as me.

We both smiled at each other: me with my battered face and Tilda in her rock'n'roll tutu. If the grey-haired woman from the coach party was still gawping, she'd be panicking now that the hooligans had joined forces to ransack the place and steal tea towels and postcards from the arms of innocent daytrippers.

Bleep!

With a wobble and a struggle, I balanced the box on one knee, wrestled my phone from my pocket, and stared at the message on the tiny screen.

Cracked the code! said the message on the tiny screen. *Got my break in 10 mins – meet me at water fountain on prom? Amber*

My heart went scrunch, and the one leg I was standing on went shaky with surprise.

"Sorry, I've got to…"

I glanced round, the sorry-I've-got-to-go still on my lips ... to find no Tilda in sight, unless you count the flutter of a black tutu disappearing between a sea of beige summer slacks...

It was fifteen minutes since Amber had said she was getting a break in ten minutes.

But it had taken time to push through the daytrippers and leave my cardboard box of treasures with one of the museum curators (along with a frantically mumbled explanation of everything I was donating).

So now I was hurrying along a little side street I hadn't been down before. I figured it was a shortcut down to the prom, and to Amber, and the secret of the curious coded message.

And as I hurried, I thought about three things:

a) What could the message possibly say?

b) What I could use to built a protective fortress round my airbed tonight? And...

b) How intrigued was I by Tilda Gilmore?

Not that I thought we could be friends or anything. Apart from Tilda being a couple of years older than me, she was hardly going to be *looking* for more friends, since she was already mates with Si and all his crew.

But then I hadn't expected to be friends with

any of the friends I'd made this summer. I mean, not long after I got to know him, TJ had stolen my phone. Rachel had been a snob who made me feel *that* big. Megan was just a holidaymaker who'd cartwheeled into me (ouch). And grumpy waitress Amber had poured a pile of pasta over my head.

Hardly written-in-the-stars starts to friendships, any of them.

In every single case though, I'd felt some strange vibes along the way, like our paths were meant to cross. Sometimes it was Peaches who seemed to be nudging me in the way of the vibes or sometimes it was something – usually bizarro – that rambly old Mrs Sticky Toffee had said when I'd bumped into her.

But let's face it, I told myself, with the sensible left-side of the brain, as I steamed breathlessly along the pavement. *Peaches might have winked a couple of times lately, but I haven't really seen anything of Mrs S-T, have I?*

Um…

Well, would you take a look at this! gloated the right-hand side of my brain.

My legs, paralysed by shock, started walking in slow motion.

'Cause there, on the other side of the road was a pretty, ivy-strewn churchyard. A churchyard where a sad-looking girl in a tutu was sitting on a bench, staring at nothing and distractedly stroking a large, vibrating, fat, ginger cat. And just behind her – though the sad-looking girl didn't seem to notice – Mrs S-T stood smiling, and feeding what looked like custard creams to a large, flapping seagull, perched on the edge of a gravestone.

It would have made sense to go over there. Well, first off, the cat *was* mine; secondly, I knew the old lady and the psycho seagull pretty well; and thirdly, Tilda Gilmore might or might not (though probably *would*, considering the signs) be my future friend.

But it was all too spooky, and my frightened legs suddenly speeded up and carried me off towards the prom at a zillion miles an hour...

Chapter 8

Pfop! Bbbbbffffffffzzzzzzzz. . .

So Peaches was a wanderer and turned up all over Portbay (and even Sugar Bay, when he was in the mood for a long hike).

So, he just *happened* to be in the churchyard, and being a cat that appreciates a cuddle, he chanced his luck and nuzzled up beside Tilda on the bench.

So, Mrs Sticky Toffee was an old lady out for a stroll, who just *happened* to stop in the peaceful churchyard, where she started feeding the birds.

It was that simple, wasn't it?

Yeah, *right*.

Me thinking about Tilda, Peaches and Mrs Sticky Toffee, and seeing them all a second later ... it must have been about the zillionth very eerie coincidence to come my way since I'd moved to Portbay. Back in London, the only regular coincidence to happen was that two number 24 buses might turn up at the stop at the same time.

Strange, strange, strange…

But it was hard putting it into words; me thinking that my cat was psychic and that there was freakiness round every corner in Portbay.

Which was why I'd never come out and said as much to my new friends. Maybe they'd think I was mad. Or maybe I didn't say anything because Rachel hadn't much liked the weird turns she'd been having since her seizures, and probably didn't want to hear any more about spooky stuff. Or maybe I hadn't told any of them because they were from Portbay and probably *knew* it was freaky without me having to say so.

All of this was wafting around in my mind as I hurried along towards the old Victorian water fountain on the prom, where I could see Amber, TJ and Rachel waiting for me. Close by, Ellie was tap-dancing with Bob looking on; her mesmerized audience of one.

"What took you so long?" Rachel called out as I got closer.

"Got stuck talking to one of the museum people," I explained, deciding not to mention the very eerie coincidence on the way.

"Yeah, well, now you're here – listen to this!" said TJ, pointing to a shyly pleased-with-herself Amber, clutching a familiar A4 sheet to her chest.

"Go on, then." I grinned at her. "I can't wait!"

"OK – here goes: *HEY ... F1 – IF ... I ... DID ... NOT ... KNOW ... BETTER ... I ... MIGHT ... THINK ... YOU ... WERE ... AVOIDING ... ME. DON'T ... YOU ... WANT ... TO ... PLAY ... OUR ... GAME ... ANY ... MORE?*"

I watched as Amber's finger trailed over the various circles, squares, triangles and squiggles she was translating.

"How do you get all that from these doodles?" I frowned.

"'Cause it's an alphabet, like Ellie said," Amber replied.

"Aflabet!" Ellie giggled, holding up an ice cream that was practically as big as her head, before getting stuck into eating it, while Bob waited patiently for drips.

TJ ruffled his sister's hair proudly, till it looked like windswept blonde candyfloss. I guessed he'd probably splashed out on the ice cream as a reward for Ellie being such an ace code breaker. She might be into tap-dancing and singing cartoon theme tunes *now*, but maybe she had a future in some secret army intelligence unit.

"OK, so it's an alphabet. But how did you work it out?" I asked, thinking it all sounded as complicated as the sort of maths that makes your palms sweat.

"You look for what must be little words, with one, two or three letters," said Amber, "'cause those are going to be stuff like 'a', 'to', 'of', 'the', and 'and'. Got that?"

I nodded, *trying* to get it.

"Once you've cracked the little words, that helps you figure out *other* words, and you start to see the alphabet. Look!"

Amber pulled a folded-up piece of paper from the pocket of her apron and flipped it open … revealing a long list of squiggles, all lined up against bits of the usual "aflabet".

"So that circle with a dot in the middle is an E?" I muttered, glancing down the list. "And that thing like a tadpole is a B?"

"Exactly." Amber nodded. "Anyway, there's still a bit more … do you want me to read it?"

Did I want her to read it? Um … let me think.

"Yes! Of *course*!!"

"*BUT … DON'T … FORGET – NO ONE … KNOWS … YOU … LIKE … I … DO … SO … WRITE … BACK … TO … ME … SOON … I'LL … KEEP … WATCHING … OUT … FOR … YOUR … MESSAGE … F2.*"

"Pretty good, huh?" said TJ, raising his eyebrows in my direction.

"The only bits that confused me were the

names," said Amber. "But it's definitely F1 and F2 – that thing that's like a triangular lollipop is definitely an F, and the numbers are just like they normally are."

"Wonder what that stands for?" I said, wondering what *all* of it stood for.

"Y'know, I thought maybe you should show it to that journalist girl at the newspaper, Stella," said TJ. "Bet she'd love to write about it, and maybe someone will come forward and say they're F1 or F2."

"Yeah, and tell everyone the story behind the message!" Rachel joined in.

"Good idea…"

I was nodding as I took the message and decoded alphabet from Amber, but funnily enough, I didn't feel like it was a good idea at all, though I had absolutely no idea why…

I was lying back in a warm, squelching puddle of mud, feeling Bob's peaches-'n'-cream-scented breath on my face. I noticed that his fur was clipped back from his eyes with a pair of diamanté dragonflies. He felt very, very heavy as he padded on my chest.

"DON'T YOU WANT TO PLAY OUR GAME ANY MORE?" he woofed at me.

"Please, you're sort of squashing me, Bob..." I groaned.

Pins of pain suddenly woke me up from my dream.

"Peaches! *Yeow!*" I whispered, lifting my fat cat far enough into the air to stop him clawing my chest to shreds with feline love.

"Prrrrrrrrr..." purred Peaches, as I squidged over on my squelchy airbed and let him share part of it.

A pair of plugged-in moon and star nightlights cast just enough of a glow for me to get a glimpse of my watch – it was nearly midnight. I hadn't seen anything of Peaches since this afternoon in the churchyard.

"Where have you been?" I whispered, so I didn't wake the demon twins.

Peaches purred and padded, purred and padded, staring at me serenely through wouldn't-you-like-to-know? slitted eyes.

"I saw you with Tilda. Did you follow her home or something?"

Prr, pad, prrrr, pad, prrrr, pad...

"Look – I know this is stupid, but can I just show you something?"

Reaching over to where my jeans lay in a crumpled pile on the floor, I wriggled my fingers around in one of the back pockets until they grabbed hold of folded-up paper.

"This is a secret message. See?" I said in a teeny-tiny voice, holding the two sheets of paper up in front of those inscrutably slanted eyes.

Peaches' whiskers twitched, as if some psychic vibes were transmitting from them.

And then he sniffed the paper and purred...

Wow, result! Er, unless, of course the paper smelled of the tuna sandwich I'd had for lunch right after I'd left Amber. *Urgh*.

"Look – if you know anything about this, like who wrote it, or what the stuff in the message is all about, then can you give me *some* sort of sign?"

Pfop!

Bbbbbffffffffffffzzzzzzzzzzzzzzzz...

Peaches' claw puncturing the airbed was a sign all right.

A sign that I'd be really uncomfortable for the rest of the night...

Chapter 9

Cats know more than they let on

It was one of those vaguely dissatisfying mornings where you start things and then stop them.

I'd come out to the den, thinking I'd get my art stuff out and make a dumb, sparkly "Welcome back!!" banner for Megan out of leftover lining paper and paint. But then I'd got my drawing pen out and started on the Tilda-esque ninja fairy that had been hovering in my head for the last couple of days. And then halfway through a wing, my mind meandered off on a tangent again, and I found myself doodling the least useful family tree ever on a blank sheet of my sketch pad. It went like this:

Joseph Grainger (born 1830-ish), married to ???
then a line down to...
Daughter ????, married in 1870/80-ish??

It wasn't exactly a long, detailed and fascinating account of Joseph's life and family. Thank goodness Frankie distracted me by phoning up all the way from London for a natter.

"Where did you hear that?"

"I read it somewhere. Dunno where," said Frankie, matter-of-factly.

Frankie knew how weird Peaches was – she'd met him when she visited at the beginning of the summer holidays, and I'd been sending her all my news via e-mail attachments over the last few weeks.

Which is why I'd been blabbering on to her about what had happened in the last day (and night) when she called my mobile just now. To which she'd said very wisely, "Well, cats know more than they let on."

While she spoke, my eyes scanned the shelves which looked half-empty since I'd dropped off the stuff to the museum. I mean, there were still all the twisty bits of driftwood and shells I'd collected, plus framed photos of my friends back in London. There was also the VIP (Very Important Photo) – since it was the only one I had – of my long-dead Granny Jones and her boyfriend Eddie (my long-lost grandad), back when they were love-struck teenagers.

Plus there were all my paints and my drawing pens, as well as a couple of the caricatures I used to like doodling, and all the funky ninja fairies I preferred doing now. Speaking of art, the cheque

I'd got for fifty pounds from Rachel's mum was pinned to my cork noticeboard. I'd have to think of something really excellent to put that towards. A new blow-up bed, maybe? I'd had to creep downstairs with my duvet in the early hours and sleep on one of the two living-room sofas. (Not as comfy as it sounds – I forgot it wasn't as wide as a bed and rolled off it in my sleep. Bad enough, except I landed on a toy dumper truck – *ooof*...)

"So anyway, when are we going to see you again, Stella?" asked Frankie, changing the subject, and putting on the sort of whiny-sad "but I really *want* that!" voice three year olds use to blackmail their mums into buying them Chocolate Buttons.

"I don't know..." I said wistfully.

The shadow of a big fat cat suddenly fell across the sunlit shelves of the den. Peaches was teetering on the narrow window ledge of the small window, blocking out the sunshine and the view of the overgrown garden with his general large furriness.

"But when you first said you were moving there," Frankie chattered on, oblivious to the green-eyed stare I was getting, "your mum and dad said you'd come back for visits to London all the time!"

Yep, I remembered Mum and Dad saying that too. But I'd also overheard them talking recently about how much money the house was swallowing, how little they had left in the bank, and how one or both of them was going to have to get organized and get a job sooner than they'd planned. So I was pretty sure family trips to London came low down on the priority list after house renovations, food and nappies.

"Well, I'll ask them and see, I s'pose."

And have them tell me that there was more chance of aliens *really* zapping a crop circle in our garden than the Stansfield family affording a weekend in a London hotel…

"Stella, your Auntie V wants to ask you a quick – oh, sorry!"

Mum – with one twin on her hip and the other wrapped round her left leg – had hauled open the door of the den and handed the house phone to me before she'd spotted that I was on my mobile.

"No – it's fine," I said hurriedly. "Frankie, can I call you back?"

"Sure," said Frankie, and I could practically see her do her usual "whatever" shrug.

I took the house phone from Mum, before she very firmly shut the door (i.e. before Jake and

Jamie could register all the interesting things they could get their hands on and break in my den).

"Auntie V? It's me!"

For most of my thirteen years, Auntie V had, well, sort of *scared* me. Not 'cause she stormed around waving axes or anything; just because she was super-elegant and super-confident ... and super-ordinary and super-shy me never knew what to say to her. But we'd kind of bonded back when my parents announced we were moving to Portbay, mainly because me and Auntie V both thought it was an insane idea at the time.

"Hey, Stella, my little star!" she said brightly. "This is just a quickie – one of my clients has just been offered a part in a new musical set in a laundrette or something equally dismal, and I've got to get the contracts in the post for him asap…"

My Auntie V hardly ever let a sentence pass by without getting a bit of sarcasm in somewhere. But I knew she loved her job (as an actors' agent), and I knew she adored her London life (in a small but very chic flat in a posh area).

"So what's up?" I asked her, at the same time moving my forefinger very slowly towards the den window, and the cat loitering on the other side of it. It's usually a very entertaining trick to play on cats – the closer your finger gets to their nose, the more cross-eyed they get. But Peaches didn't seem to be falling for it; he just carried on staring straight at me.

"Well, your mum was just talking about the holidays ending next week and how you'll be starting at your new school…"

Flip! went my stomach with a hiccup of nerves at the very idea.

"…and I suddenly thought, how would you like to come and spend your *next* school holiday here with me in London? Just you and me, I mean? We could do some things together, and you could catch up with your old friends too."

Frankie was right – cats know more than they let on. And Peaches had known that there was a coincidence brewing, you could tell by the way he was almost smirking at me now.

"Yes! I mean, yes, please!" I blustered, mentally trying to count how many weeks it would be till the October break. "But how will I—"

"Get here?" Auntie V pre-empted me. "Your mum and dad will put you on a train there, and I'll come and pick you up!"

Ker-thunk! went my stomach with *more* than a hiccup of nerves.

But then that's exactly what was happening with Megan this weekend… I'd have to ask her how it felt to be on your own travelling on quite a long journey. Nerve-wracking? (I'd be scared the train re-routed to Carlisle and stranded me there.) Exciting? (Being on your own, like an independent adult – for three hours anyway...)

"Great! We'll talk about it more, nearer the time. Got to go... Bye!"

"Bye! And, uh, thanks!"

But she was already gone.

"OK – you can stop staring at me now!" I said, grinning at Peaches through the glass. "I get the coincidence!"

The loud *bringgggg!* of the phone in my hand made me jump – but Peaches (cool cat that he is) didn't twitch a ginger hair on his body.

"Hello?"

"Is that Stella?"

"Yes," I replied, trying to place the voice.

"It's Jane from the *Portbay Journal* – I thought I'd call and let you know we've had some interesting news to do with Joseph!"

"Yeah?" I said, intrigued.

"Mmm. It seems that an older gentleman paid a visit to the museum yesterday – and identified the setting of Joseph's portrait there. He recognized the building as an old dairy that used to stand in the village of Somerton, about fifteen miles from here. Do you know Somerton?"

"No, I don't," I told her. Dad was so busy with the house and Mum was so busy with my brothers that we hadn't done any sightseeing since we'd been here. I'd gone to the nearest town – Westbay – with Rachel and her mum once, but that was it for my local knowledge outside of Portbay.

"And that's not all. The curator went on to show the gentleman the photo of Joseph at his daughter's wedding – and the church is in Somerton too, so that's obviously where Joseph settled. That's all we've got to go on just now, but it's a good start. I just thought you'd be keen to hear about it."

I was – and I was grateful that someone with a job as important as a journalist would take time to phone little old me. I was very grateful, and wished I had a way of showing my thanks, rather than just saying a wimpy thank you.

And then my eyes strayed to the coded letter and aflabet that were laid out on the desk in front of me. That was it…! TJ had said I should tell Jane about it; it could be a great story for her.

"Thanks for letting me know," I began to say, "and there's something else…"

I'd just gone to pick up the two sheets of paper in front of me when a funny ginger leg shot through the one pane-less section of window and firmly fixed them back down on to the desk with four sharp claws.

"Sorry? What was that?" said Jane.

"Um, nothing. No. It's, uh, just good to hear the stuff about Joseph," I mumbled.

For some reason I hadn't been able to figure out, I wasn't that keen on the idea of telling Jane about the message when TJ had suggested it. And now it looked like Peaches was sure it wasn't a fantastic idea either.

And you know what they say, cats know more than they let on…

Chapter 10

The amazing small adventure plan

There was a beautiful halo of red-golden light around Amber's head. If she'd been wearing old-fashioned clothes, she could have easily looked like some romantic heroine in a painting from … well, whenever they painted romantic heroines with halos of light around their heads.

"She was in here earlier, with a photographer," Amber chatted, moving slightly so that the halo disappeared and her ginger hair wasn't backlit by the new chilli pepper fairy lights on the café wall any more. "They were taking pictures of the new look, for a story in the paper."

Amber was talking about Jane the journalist, as she hovered beside our table, on duty but with no customers in need of her attention (for now). Her new uniform was very cute – cut-off jeans with turn-ups, white trainers, white T-shirt and a bright orange apron with a red chilli pepper printed on it.

"I wish Phil hadn't made me be in the photo," Amber continued. "I hope it's black and white, so they don't see how much I was blushing…"

When Amber was in full flush-blush mode her pink cheeks *did* clash a bit with her red hair. But with so many colours competing for centre stage in the newly decorated Hot Pepper Jelly café, I didn't think the newspaper readers of Portbay would pay her cheeks *that* much attention. Except for maybe Tilda; *she* might be tempted to draw a few spots and a beard on Amber's face, the way she seemed to feel about her.

"Hey, I was thinking," TJ suddenly burst out, with his Coke halfway to his mouth, "we could all go there! Easy!"

"Go where easy?" asked Ellie, looking up from the blueberry muffin she was breaking up into a pile of crumbs on her plate.

"Somerton!" TJ answered her briskly. "Bet we could probably find out loads about Joseph on our own!"

"But how would we get there?" I asked.

"Bus?" TJ shrugged. "Well, two – we'd have to take one to Westbay, to the bus station there, and then swap to one that goes to Somerton."

"And I guess it could be a proper day out too… We could all take picnic stuff!" I said, feeling fired-up at the idea of finding out more about Joseph *and* doing something different with my best friends.

TJ, Rachel and Amber were all pretty excited – just like I'd been – to hear what Jane from the newspaper had had to say. Only now, Rachel and Amber *weren't* looking so excited…

"What's up?" I asked.

"I'm working every day till school starts, so I can't come," said Amber with a fed-up shrug.

"And thanks to my paranoid mother, I'm never going to be allowed out of Portbay on my own," growled Rachel. "Well, at least not till I'm forty-two and she's satisfied that I haven't had another seizure!"

I couldn't argue with work and sarcasm. But it was kind of disappointing.

"Megan'll be here on Friday – she'll be up for coming with us!" TJ said, turning to me.

He was right. *Course* Megan would be up for it. So there'd only be the three of us (and probably Ellie and Bob too), but it would still be an amazing small adventure…

Except our amazing small adventure seemed to be cancelled before it had begun.

I could tell by the look that had just flitted

between my mum and dad when I'd blurted out our plan to bus it to Somerton. A look that said, "Will you tell her, or will I? That she can't go?"

"What's wrong?" I asked, before they did that telepathic thing that parents do and decided which one was going to dole out the bad news.

"Stella, you're only thirteen," said Dad. "It's one thing to be wandering around Portbay on your own—"

"– and plenty of parents would think that's too much at your age," Mum chipped in apologetically, as if that was supposed to make me feel better.

"But going off to some far-flung village with only your friends for company – it's just not safe."

Y'know, sometimes it's a complete bummer to be thirteen and reminded of it.

"What – do you think some creep would try to abduct three teenagers, a five year old and a huge dog?" I said, using a touch of Rachel's sarcasm.

Mum and Dad both sighed and looked awkward. They weren't very good at being strict. Specially since we were in the hardware shop, supposed to be picking paint for my room and being jolly. Also, it was difficult to hold an argument in a shop where we were the only customers – we seemed to be embarrassing the shy-looking hardware shop owner, standing there in his brown overall coat, his bald head glistening slightly as he pretended to tidy up an already neat pile of hinges.

"Look, why don't we all go to this Somerton place next week sometime, when Dad's not so busy with the house?" Mum suggested brightly. "We could take a nice drive there, have a look around, stop at some old-fashioned tea shop for lunch…"

"Can't. I'm starting school next week, in case you'd forgotten," I said forlornly.

"Listen, let's talk about this later… How about we get the paint sorted out, so I can get started on it straight away, hmm?" Dad suggested.

"Good idea," said Mum too quickly. "Stella, can you keep an eye on the boys for two seconds, while I just check out those lamps over there?"

With Mum shooting off to look at lamps, and Dad lugging two pots of paint up on to the counter, I was left to mope with Jake and Jamie, who were safely strapped in their double buggy.

"Lady!" cooed Jake, sticking a chubby arm towards the window.

"Sweetie lady!" murmured Jamie, sticking a skinny arm out and now waving in the same direction.

I glanced up and saw Mrs Sticky Toffee passing by, merrily blowing kisses to the boys – and to me, I think. For a second I was torn; keen to rush outside and stop her in her pink and green tracks. Mrs S-T knew odd bits of everything about Portbay, so she probably knew odd bits of something to do with Somerton too. But I could hardly just walk out and leave the boys, specially when they were within grabbing distance of a display of tubs of glue. Course, maybe I could quickly wheel them outside… Oh, who was I kidding, you couldn't do *anything* quickly with a double buggy. It was like trying to manoeuvre a shopping trolley around a toilet cubicle. And even in the time I'd thought of that, Mrs S-T was gone.

And Tilda Gilmore was stomping along in the direction of the shop instead.

Is she really going to come in here? I wondered. What could a goth ballerina want in a hardware shop? Black paint to touch up her room? Some bin liners to use as an alternative duvet cover?

"Have you seen Xenon?!" Tilda barked out, as soon as she'd barged through the door.

She looked agitated – worried and angry, even. So worried and angry that she didn't seem to notice the existence of me or my brothers or my parents.

"I – I – don't know what you mean! I don't know *where* he is!" said the now-nervous hardware shop man (probably reaching for a panic button or a sink plunger underneath the counter if things turned nasty).

Tilda was breathing hard, and her fists were so clenched that the knuckles stood out skeleton white.

"*Thanks!*" she spat out furiously, but with a glint of a tear treacherously spilling from the corner of her eye. "Thanks for nothing, Dad!"

Dad? yelped a voice in my head as Tilda stormed out of the shop, slamming the glass-paned door behind her.

That was Tilda Gilmore's *dad*? It couldn't be. Except it could, since the sign along the counter read Gilmore's Household Supplies.

Wow.

I'd tried to picture Tilda's parents before, and I guess I'd thought her dad would be more like a Hell's Angel with a mean motorbike than a hardware salesman, doing a nice line in buckets and picture hooks.

Talk about a surprise. But now the mystery of at least one of Tilda's parents was solved, the *next* mystery was who Xenon was. A runaway older brother? A secret boyfriend?

I couldn't wait to find out. Even if I didn't know how that could possibly happen. Unless of course I asked Tilda's dad to give me an explanation, along with the receipt for the paint...

Chapter 11

The mystery of Xenon. . .

Dad had gone home to paint (woodwork first, so it wasn't too exciting).

Mum had taken the boys to the beach (she'd asked me along, but I wasn't in the mood – guess why).

Instead, I'd wandered to the library, with a vague plan of looking up some information on Somerton, since I'd been told I wasn't going there. But so far, all I'd done was amble up and down the local history section, running my finger along the spines of various books and getting a crick in my neck. I wasn't even reading the names on the spines; instead my head was whizzing in circles, thinking about Mum and Dad saying no to my amazing small adventure; musing about Tilda and her hissy fit; kicking myself for being a complete coward and not asking her dad who Xenon was. (I know it would have been incredibly cheeky of me, but it would have solved the mystery in one fell swoop.)

Tippetty-tap, tippetty-tap, tippetty-tap…

"They've brought it forward again – have you seen?" said Mr Harper the librarian, practising his tap-dancing moves while he went about his work.

I did a quick check over my shoulder and realized he *had* to be talking to me, since there were only two of us in the library on this baking hot afternoon.

"Sorry?" I said, shyly stepping towards him, and the piece of newspaper he was pinning to a noticeboard on the wall.

"Joseph's house – you're interested in that, aren't you?" he asked.

He'd spotted me here before, flicking through old books about Portbay, trying to find out anything I could about the place.

"Yes." I nodded, walking up closer.

"Well, this was just in the paper today – the demolition team are moving in on Monday. And the removal of the chandelier is happening on Friday. Cutting it fine, isn't it?"

"I can't believe it won't be there any more…" I mumbled, staring sadly at the photo, and trying to imagine how empty Sugar Bay would look without the grand old mansion standing there at the foot of the cliffs. At least how empty it would look till the building firm started work on all the identikit new holiday homes…

"Oh, I'm sure there will still be some kind of trace of it, for a while yet," said Mr Harper, tapping one foot heel-toe-heel-toe.

"A trace…?" I mumbled vaguely, not wanting to sound too stupid.

"Well, it's just that people and places sometimes leave a trace of themselves." Mr Harper smiled at me. "Like in here, there are days I'm sure I've seen someone familiar out of the corner of my eye, strolling down the aisles or browsing through a book. And then I look again and there's no one there."

"Like a ghost?" I said sharply, suddenly panicking that the library was haunted or that Mr Harper was having a breakdown.

"No, not exactly." He laughed gently. "Maybe it's more that your mind's eye can picture people or things that you're used to, and you can almost see them when you're in the right mood. Children and animals are supposed to be good at spotting traces … have you noticed the way they sometimes seem to be reacting to things that aren't there?"

Peaches freaked me out by doing that all the time. He must see a world *packed* with traces, the way he stared hard at nothing in particular on a regular basis.

"So … you're saying that I might see the house again?" I said dubiously. A trace of a house sounded pretty huge to me.

"Sure, why not? You might be walking along the headland one day, and look down at some seagulls swooping, and almost see the top of the roof, and a glint of the huge windows…"

"…and the tangled garden," I finished off, thinking that Mr Harper was either very poetic or very mad. Still, it made me want to get back to Sugar Bay soon, so I could get a good long look at Joseph's house before it was gone for good. Maybe I could go tomorrow with TJ, or on Friday with Megan once she was here.

"I suppose there'll be a few people round at the Bay to watch the demolition on Monday, sad as it'll be," said Mr Harper, taking down a "Learn To Play Ping-Pong!" poster and getting ready to pin something else on the noticeboard.

School (urgh) didn't start till Tuesday, but I didn't know if I could stand being there on the headland in the crowds, watching the smashing and crushing below – it would be too stomach-churningly miserable.

"Still, enough of me chatting – was there

anything I can help you with today?"

Mr Harper pinned a new notice up on the board with a flourish of a hand and a rat-tat-tat of his heels.

"Well, I was just looking for…"

My voice fizzled out as my eyes settled on the "LOST" poster he'd just stuck up. Whoever had asked him to put it up there hadn't lost your standard stuff, like a cat or a dog, or a mobile or house keys. They'd lost a small something with beady eyes (currently boring into mine, it felt like). A small something with a long tail. A small something called Xenon – who happened to be a rat. A rat with the tiniest kerchief I'd ever seen around its neck.

"Oh, have you seen it?" Mr Harper asked, spotting the startled expression on my face and mistaking it for recognition.

"Um, no," I said, shaking my head quickly.

So Xenon was Tilda's rat, according to this quickly made, handwritten poster.

Much missed pet, it read. *Please phone if you've seen him.*

I think it was the phone number that made a loud *ker-pow!* happen in my head. I mean, the way she'd written the numbers "1" and "2", with a swirl and a flourish … it was exactly the same as on the coded sheets of paper that had been stuck up around Portbay.

So Xenon was a rat.

And Tilda was the writer of the mystery messages; the person who signed herself "F2".

Which only left one question; who was "F1", the person the mystery messages were left for...?

Chapter 12

How to fracture a heart

Ten o'clock, Thursday morning, and the sea was looking strangely quiet.

Only a couple of surfers were out doing their surf thing. Where were the others? Maybe daytripping around the rest of Portbay, having fun snickering at the place and the people who lived here.

The sooner they packed up their surfboards and went in search of the next wave the better. Though they were probably sticking around to see themselves in the local paper, I bet...

Speaking about things being strangely quiet, the Hot Pepper Jelly wasn't exactly bustling. Though it probably wouldn't stay that way for long...

"Uh-oh, I spy a coach party!" said Amber, looking from the road outside the window down to the watch on her wrist. "Should be here in five minutes, by the time they park and wander along..."

Aw. I was quite enjoying being the only customer. Phil the owner had asked me to choose which CD to put on (they were all called stuff like "salsa" this and "Tex-Mex" that, so I picked one by a band called the Gipsy Kings 'cause the cover of the CD had some nice sunflowers on it). And Amber had put two slices of lemon in my fizzy water, *and* given me a chocolate chip cookie that I hadn't asked for ("Phil said it was fine").

Because there were no other customers, Amber had been able to hover and listen intently to my tales of yesterday. Right before her in-built waitress radar had spotted the coach just now, we'd been happily yabbering on about Tilda and the mystery messages, and trying to figure out who "F1" could be.

"Hey, Amber," I said, picking up on where we'd left our conversation, "d'you think that it might be Si Riley? The message said '*NO ONE KNOWS YOU LIKE I DO*', and they're really good friends."

I couldn't claim to be the person who came up with that idea; it was Megan by e-mail this morning, after I'd given her the gossip. (Megan was one of those people who comes over all dippy, but is actually secretly very smart when they want to be.)

"Maybe." Amber shrugged, twirling her notepad pencil around her fingers. "But then it also said, '*IF I DIDN'T KNOW BETTER, I'D THINK YOU WERE AVOIDING ME*', and that doesn't fit, 'cause her and Si and all their other mates are in here all the time."

"Oh, yeah..." I nodded, disappointed that Megan's ace suggestion turned out to be a bit like trying to squash a round peg into a square hole.

"Hi, Amber! Can I get a quick egg roll before I have to go to work?"

As Si Riley bustled into the café – with his record bag draped over his shoulder and looking like a member of some alternative rock band – Amber dropped her pencil on the floor with a clatter and went bright pink. I wasn't much better; to hide my embarrassment about nearly getting caught talking about him, I took too big a bite of my cookie and started choking.

"You guys all right?" he frowned at us both.

"Oh, you know, just..." Amber fizzled out, as pathetic as *I* was at coming up with spontaneous lies.

"Uh-oh, *hide* me..." Si said suddenly, oblivious to our feeble excuses and choking now that something had attracted his attention outside the window. He positioned himself right behind

Amber, resting his hands on her waist so she couldn't move.

"Um, what's up?" asked Amber, looking down warily at Si's hands, and blushing furiously.

"Tilda," Si hissed, staring at a tutu'd figure across the road, just visible through the regular prom-parading traffic and ambling summer strollers.

"Tilda? But so what? She's your mate!" said Amber, fanning her face with her notepad.

(I was letting her do the talking, since she and Si had become buddies lately. I was suddenly very aware of being only thirteen in front of a seventeen-year-old MTV star lookalike.)

"Well, *yeah*..." replied Si, not sounding very convincing. "It's just that she's been getting a bit much lately, with that stuff she's been sticking up."

OK – I was going to jump in at this point, since I instantly recognized the sheet of paper Tilda was currently taping to the lamp-post across the road.

"It's a lost poster – her rat's gone missing," I told him.

"What, *Xenon*? Yeah? What a bummer!" muttered Si, peeking out from the side of Amber. "I thought she was putting up another of these messages she leaves round town for me..."

I locked eyes with Amber for a flicker of a

moment, wondering if we should let him know that we knew.

"Er, what messages are those, then?" Amber asked Si, quickly breaking our eye-lock.

(Probably just as well she did that, or we might have seemed like crazed stalkers to him.)

"It's just something dumb we came up with one time, when I was working in the Vault and she came and hung out. We made up a secret language, and decided to leave messages up for each other around Portbay. Stuff no one else could understand, just for the buzz."

"Oh... I think I might have seen one of those," said Amber, trying to sound casual but going telltale pink all over again. Si didn't notice; he was too busy holding on to Amber's waist and peeking at Tilda from his hiding place.

"Yeah, it was a laugh for a while," he carried on, "just writing stuff about bands we liked, or telling jokes, and then it all started to get a bit heavy. It's just ... well, I don't mean to sound big-headed, but they sort of started sounding like she ... well, like she had a *crush* on me or whatever. So I've been trying not to be on my own with her –"

(*IF I DIDN'T KNOW BETTER, I'D THINK YOU WERE AVOIDING ME*, zapped through my head.)

"– and I haven't written any back to her in ages –"

(*DON'T YOU WANT TO PLAY OUR GAME ANY MORE?*)

"– 'cause I'm hoping she kind of takes the hint without me having to say it out loud, if you get me."

"What – that you don't fancy her?" Amber came out and asked, tilting her head round to face him.

"God, *no*! Tilda's cool and everything, but I know my mates think she's a bit intense and screwy. They only put up with her for my sake. I mean, if they knew about all this, they'd rip the –"

I had a feeling Si was just about to say something very rude when he stopped dead.

I glanced out of the window and across the road – and saw Tilda break into a smile and a wave as she spotted her so-called friend. And then the smile faded as she also spotted whose waist he seemed to have his arms around.

Tilda tried to turn and run, but she'd been in the middle of taping the "LOST" poster up and had to suffer the indignity of being stuck for a second, till she yanked hard and ended up hurrying along the prom with the sheet of paper attached to her hand and flapping in the breeze like a rubbish, home-made bonsai kite.

"Wow. What happened there?" asked Si, gazing into Amber's face for an answer. (Being only thirteen, I was obviously invisible to him, and so he didn't even bother thinking I might have the answer.)

With her face flushing as pink as strawberry milkshake with too much strawberry syrup added to it, Amber shuffled her feet in her new trainers and fidgeted with her notepad and pencil.

"I think you're right," she said finally. "I think Tilda *does* have a crush on you. And – and I think she's kind of jealous of us talking ... or getting on ... or whatever. I think she thinks ... well, *y'know*. Although we're *not*, obviously."

Poor Amber... It's very hard trying to let someone know that you don't fancy them, without it sounding like you're hiding the fact that you secretly do. Which she didn't, if you see what I mean.

"No! No, course not!" Si frowned, dropping his hands from Amber's waist and rubbing them through his gelled, spiky black (and purple) hair. "We're just mates too! But you know something? It's kind of perfect if Tilda thinks that... It'll maybe get her off my back!"

Amber looked half-pleased to be helpful in

some way to Si, and half-horrified at the idea of being used as an excuse to keep Tilda at bay.

As for Tilda ... all I could think was thank Peaches that I didn't hand over the coded messages to Jane the reporter after all. At the moment, Tilda was suffering from a severe fracture of the heart, I was sure, and the idea of her unrequited love being splashed across the local paper would have been too mortifyingly awful to imagine.

"Omigod – I'm so late, I'm going to be fired," mumbled Si, checking out the time and hauling his record bag on to his shoulder. "Oh, by the way – there's a beach party happening round in Sugar Bay on Saturday, starting around six-ish. Me and my mates are all going. Fancy it?"

"Mmm!" Amber mumbled non-committally, with a shrug, as Si tried to leave.

Hmm... I had a feeling that that invite wasn't particularly directed at me, since Si seemed incapable of registering the existence of anyone less than two years younger than him.

Whatever ... getting out of the Hot Pepper Jelly was harder than a very cool, seventeen-year-old alt-rocker might've expected, thanks to a coachload of ravenous grannies, anxious for a scone and pot of tea.

And all thoughts of the invitation Si had just flung her seemed to vanish temporarily from Amber's mind as panic set in.

"Don't fancy learning how to be a waitress – *fast* – do you?" Amber asked in my direction, looking daunted.

"Sorry, got stuff to do," I told her, heading for the door myself, and wondering if perhaps a psycho seagull, a batty old lady or a waft of peaches 'n' cream might lead me to wherever Tilda Gilmore had vanished to…

Chapter 13

A skewed coincidence (or two)

Si Riley's mates thought that Tilda was too intense, and too screwy.

So why would Rachel or TJ or Amber think any differently? Specially since they all knew by now what *I* knew; that Tilda had written the coded messages with Si, only hers had gotten slightly too clingy for (Si's) comfort. Even easygoing Megan was going to take a bit of convincing, since Tilda hadn't exactly been friendly with Amber *ever*, never mind since she'd got it in her head that something was going on between Amber and Si Riley.

Y'know, that stupid notion I recently had that Tilda might one day be part of our little gang...? It was nuts. Plain, ready-salted *nuts*...

"Tilda's probably back at her house, making a wax effigy of Si or Amber to stick pins into," TJ's voice buzzed into my ear.

He was at his flat with Ellie, merrily taking the

mick out of what I'd told him had just happened, completely unaware that I was wandering the streets of Portbay, hoping to catch a glimpse of a tutu.

"Either that, or she's back at Madame Xara's for another spook lesson," he chatted on. "Voodoo for beginners… Spells for work-experience witches…"

I'd forgotten we'd seen Tilda going into Madame Xara's shop the other day. Maybe I should take a detour round there, instead of ambling through the back streets.

"Hubble, bubble," TJ croaked in a pathetic attempt to sound like a witch. "Toil and troub— Ellie! *Don't* put your tap shoes on Bob! Huh? Because he doesn't like the noise and they don't suit him! Sorry, Stella, I've got to go before Bob chews off these stupid shoes…"

"That's OK, I've got to go too," I said quickly, turning a corner and spying someone I *really* wanted to talk to. They might not be in a tutu, but they'd do.

Mrs Sticky Toffee was tottering along the pavement towards me, her head bent down as she rifled in her tiny, shiny cream handbag.

"What *have* I done with it… Now where could it be in here…" she was muttering to herself.

"Um, hello!" I said, loudly enough to attract

her attention but not so loud as to startle her. As my Auntie V once told me, startling old people is as bad as pulling faces at babies and making them cry.

"Oh, hello dear," said Mrs S-T, coming to a stop without looking up at me.

Her handbag seemed crammed to the rafters, as usual. Spilling out of the top was the corner of a bulging packet of sweets, a lace-edged hankie, part of a long French loaf, and even the handle of an umbrella (it could only be a handle – the bag was so tiny there was nowhere else for even the smallest of umbrellas to go).

"Lost something?" I asked.

"Just my mind, dear!" she laughed good-naturedly. "Toffee?"

Her delicately boned hand passed me a toffee before diving back in for a further rummage.

"Thank you," I said, untwirling the wrapper. "Er… I've been *hoping* to bump into you, actually."

"Have you, dear? How nice!"

Mrs S-T glanced up for a second and blasted a sweet smile my way.

"It's just that I found out some more about Joseph, from the big house… He ended up living and working in a village near here, called Somerton. Do you know it?"

"Somerton? Oh, yes. Some of my family are from around there. Nice enough place, but I couldn't be doing with living there. It's stuck right in the middle of the countryside. Not like Portbay – no beach, no sea, no view. No thanks!"

Mrs S-T was sounding very offhand … which seemed a bit weird, seeing as she'd been the one who helped get me wondering about the history of Joseph and the house and the Grainger family in the first place. Somehow I thought she'd be a bit more interested. But the only thing that seemed to be holding her interest was searching for whatever she'd lost.

"I'd still quite like to go there sometime," I said, trying again. "Just to see where Joseph spent his life."

Actually, I'd've quite liked to go there straight away, whether my parents wanted me to or not. But to do that, I'd have to be brave and rebellious. And brave and rebellious weren't two traits I could call my own (shy and sensible were more like it). Plus there was the little problem to do with the fact that I really liked my mum and dad, and even if I didn't go along with their decision about the planned day trip to Somerton, I couldn't break their trust.

"Yes, well, that might be a nice trip, but I wouldn't bother," said Mrs S-T, taking out a giant set of keys, a ball of blue wool and a pack of tissues and handing them to me. "Can you hold these for a second?"

"Why?"

"Oh, because I'm just looking for something and there's so much of everything in my way…"

"Uh, no – I meant, why shouldn't I bother?"

"Going to Somerton?" said Mrs S-T absently, as she took back the keys, wool and the tissues and stuffed them in her raincoat pockets. "Oh, because you'd probably be better off staying here."

"I don't – I don't really understand…"

"Well, what is it that Dorothy in *The Wizard of Oz* says? 'There's no place like home. There's no place like home!'"

Ah, Mrs S-T… Conversations with her wouldn't be the same if they made sense. She was probably right; she probably *was* losing her mind.

"Here it is! I *knew* I had it in here somewhere!" she suddenly announced, pulling what looked like a card out of her bag. "I picked this up in a second-hand shop or somewhere, and thought of you, since you like art so much."

"Thank you," I said, taking the worn, stiff, folded paper she was holding out to me.

"Must dash – have got fairy cakes to make. Bye, dear!"

With a wave of her fingers she was off, humming "Somewhere Over the Rainbow" and leaving my heart a-flutter at the obviously hand-drawn card in my hand. It was a pen-and-ink image of Joseph's house, in simple outline, but with a vivid greeny-blue dragonfly darting in the foreground, painted in watercolour. And just behind the house was an orange sun so vivid, it almost looked like the flames that the real sun was made of.

I opened the crackling paper and read the inscription, written in swirly, old-fashioned lettering.

Greetings on your 21st birthday, my dearest Violet. With fond thoughts, Elize Grainger. May 28th, 1901.

I knew I'd recognized the style of the drawing as soon as I saw it. And the year Elize did it – 1901 – that meant she was already living in the house that was now ours. She'd retired there in 1900, when she'd finally had to give up on the big house, when her money ran out and she couldn't afford to keep patching it up any more.

So who was Violet? I wondered, right before my mind started racing on to other thoughts, like how amazing it was to have something else of Elize's, and how kind it was of Mrs S-T to give it to me, and how ... er ... wait a minute, let me get this right; Mrs S-T was looking for it in her bag *before* she even *saw* me?

How did *that* work...?

A couple of minutes' walk away from home, I picked up a text from Frankie, saying she'd been shopping for new school shoes in Oxford Street this morning, and was in a complete dilemma, 'cause she couldn't decide whether to go for flats or wedges.

Ha!

The dilemmas in *my* head this morning were so complicated they'd never fit on a text message back.

I mean, what was with the skewed coincidence? What *had* made Mrs S-T rifle around in her bag for that card, when she didn't even know I was around the corner? Was that nice old lady with her wobbly pink meringue of a hat and sensible raincoat more of a witch than screwy and spooky Tilda Gilmore?

"Andy! *Anddddeeee!* I can't find any!" Mum was yelling up the stairs when I walked in. She was obviously trying to do seventeen things at once; apart from yelling up the stairs to my dad, she had a bundle of wet washing tucked under her left arm and a potty clasped in her right hand, as well as the phone tucked in one of the back pockets of her jeans, and a tomato-sauce-covered wooden spoon sticking out of the other.

"Don't worry, Lou! I found some!" I heard Dad's voice yell down from the vicinity of my bedroom.

"What's up?" I asked my harassed-looking mum. I wondered if she knew she had a squiggle of blue pen down her face and on to her white vest top. (The work of a non-artistic toddler for sure.)

"Nothing. Well, nothing *much*," Mum said with a quick wince. "Your dad just kicked over a pot of white gloss paint and was trying to find some white spirit to clear it up."

There's no place like home – especially MY *disastrous home*, I thought, *sort* of quoting Mrs S-T, who in turn had been quoting Dorothy from *The Wizard of Oz*. And at this rate, I was going to need help from the wonderful, wonderful wizard of Oz if I was going to stand the remotest chance of having a semi-habitable room for Megan and the supposed girly sleepover tomorrow night.

"Are you all right, Stella?" Mum asked

hesitantly, obviously worried I was still mad at her and Dad. But now I wasn't so much mad at them as confused by the rambling riddles Mrs S-T spoke in.

"Mmm, fine." I shrugged. "Think I'll just go out to the den for a while."

All of a sudden, I was quite in the mood to get back to my Tilda-styled fairy drawing.

"Oh, I nearly forgot, Stella – there was a message for you. Hold this…"

What was with today? I kept being asked to hold things. And right now, I'd rather have held the damp washing than the full potty, but then Mum looked so frazzled that I was just glad she'd been together enough to take a message for me at all.

"I scribbled it down," she muttered, pulling a piece of paper out of her back pocket and expertly unfolding it with one hand. "Let's see… A carton of milk and some nappy sacks. Nope, that's not it."

With a flick of the wrist, she turned the paper over and seemed to struggle to understand her rushed squiggles. Maybe I needed to get Ellie and Amber in to decipher again.

"Ah, yes… Jane from the newspaper rang. She says there's some more news on Joseph. The inscription on the park bench that you came across; they've checked with the local council, and it was put on in 1949. The council did a lot of brightening up work around town in the few years after the war, and new benches and dedications were part of that."

"Yeah? That's really cool to know…" I mused.

"Yes, but there's more. Apparently, local parish details in Somerton show that Joseph was married to a woman named Grace Barnes in 1859, and they went on to have a daughter called Letty –"

"The bride in the wedding photo," I muttered, trying to take in all these new strands of info in the rambling tangle of history to do with Joseph.

Joseph Grainger (born 1830-ish), married to Grace Barnes – I rewrote the scribbled family tree in my head. Then there was a line down to…

Daughter Letty, married in 1870/80-ish to…

Who knows, I said to myself, stopping dead.

"Well, very probably," Mum agreed with what I'd said out loud. "And it seems that Letty and her husband – a Frank Harding, I think it says here, had a daughter, born in 1880, called… I can't read my own writing! Oh, yes – Violet."

Wow! I thought, instantly remembering the name of the ancient birthday message on the card

Mrs Sticky Toffee gave me, and amending the doodled family tree yet again.

Letty, married Frank Harding...

And a line came down from that to...

Violet, born 1880.

At my old school in London, I made my maths teacher very, very weary, due to the fact that maths came as easily to me as ballet dancing in concrete wellies. But he'd have been so proud of me then, working out in pretty much a nano-second that Violet would have been sixty-nine in 1949, and may well have been the granddaughter who'd arranged the dedication for him. Maybe she settled in Portbay, and as an old man he came to visit her, and they'd go for walks up there in Palladium Park...

Y'know, there'd been so many coincidences today that I could have done with a lie down – *if* I'd had a proper bed to lie down in, instead of an airbed repaired with a bike puncture kit. Still, the shrill screaming of the twins outside right now would've woken the dead (never mind me) with a jolt.

"What've they done?!" Mum gasped, bolting outside with the washing unravelling in a soggy, dropped line of tea towels and boy socks behind her.

I bolted too, expecting to see Jake trying to eat a stone or Jamie trying to lasso (i.e. strangle) his brother with the washing line.

"Where are they?" Mum asked in a panic, as the garden showed no trace of boys, stung, strangled or otherwise. "JAKE! JAMIE!!"

"Bet I know where they are," I muttered, bounding through the scratchy long grass towards our mini crop circle.

And there they were, two small boys in the oasis TJ had made, dressed in soggy nappies, tomato-stained T-shirts and both pointing, hypnotized.

"Stewwa! Look!!" shrieked Jamie, suddenly realizing I was there.

"*Naughty* cat!" yelped an indignant Jake – poking an indignant fat finger in the direction of Peaches, who was sitting zen-like in the middle of the circle.

"No… *Clever* cat," I corrected my brother, as I stepped into the circle, bent forward and studied the rat – wearing a weeny kerchief – that was swinging upside-down trapeze style, with its tail held firmly in Peaches' mouth. All four little legs were pedalling the air, but it was going nowhere fast.

"Nice to meet you, Xenon," I said softly, as Peaches let go of his prize and allowed me to scoop the rat into my cradled hands.

Since this morning, I'd been wishing I could somehow cheer Tilda up, and it seemed like I'd just found a way...

Chapter 14

Another twist, another turn

"Oh, Mr Noodles!" we heard Tilda coo in a whisper. "I've missed you *so* much!"

Mr Noodles? TJ mouthed at me, eyes wide and a grin even wider on his face.

It seemed like the mighty Xenon had a cuddlier nickname at home.

I'd found out where exactly Tilda's home was from Rachel, who'd phoned her brother at the Vault and asked for the address. I'd thought Rachel might come with me, but she said she wasn't going to go anywhere *near* a rat, even one safely stowed in a shoebox (with airholes punched in the lid, of course). But TJ was well up for being my moral support – specially when his mum wasn't working for once and had let him off babysitting duties with Ellie. *And* because he wanted a nosey at Tilda's room to see if it really was painted witchy black.

It was.

And with purple voile curtains at the window, it was so dark that it was hard to make out the blacky-brown hairy splodge of Bob sprawled on the floor. Only his panting helped pinpoint the fact that he was lying over near the door.

But the arty gloom of Tilda's bedroom was still quite a shock after walking into her tidy council house, with its floral curtains at the window, matching floral wallpaper inside, smiley, floral-skirted mum and the overpowering floral waft of a Glade Plug-In or three.

Surprisingly, for a room painted black, there were flowers in Tilda's room too – well, at least there were flowers on the amazing posters on her walls. Four big posters, all drawn by the same artist, of different statuesque women draped in so many garlands of magnolia and old rose that you could practically smell them.

"I think my aunt has one of these in her flat," I said, suddenly realizing why they looked so familiar.

Everything on Auntie V's walls had something to do with the theatre. The poster she had like these was of some old stage actress from for ever ago.

"Alphonse Mucha – that's the name of the artist," said Tilda, without glancing up from her beloved Xenon/Mr Noodles, who was now getting snuggled to death in her arms. The box I'd carried him in was lying discarded on the rug, next to a row of near-identical Doc Marten boots. (Each pair had a mini-makeover of different coloured laces or painted flowers and dragonflies on them.)

I noticed TJ's nose was wrinkled up as he gawped at the posters. Not only were they a bit too girly for him, but I was pretty sure he thought they were too girly for Tilda too. I suppose we'd *both* thought scary musicians like Marilyn Manson and Slipknot might be staring down at us, all freakshow and horror.

But then just like I'd sort of suspected, there seemed to be a soft centre to Tilda. There was the Mr Noodles business, of course. And a couple of minutes ago, when TJ had picked up a pile of cool *Ghost World* comics from Tilda's bookshelf, I'd spotted the whole collection of *Little House on the Prairie* books. And it might have been tied on to her bedpost with black ribbon, but that was still a well-loved old teddy dangling there…

A blast of daylight and a tinkle of cups made us all jump.

"Whoops-a-daisy!" giggled Tilda's mum, bustling in in a waft of too-sweet perfume and pink lipstick and nearly tripping over Bob. "Just some tea and biscuits, to say thank you for finding Xenon!"

"Thanks, Mum," Tilda smiled up at her, just as me and TJ mumbled our thanks too.

Y'know, me and my mum don't look much like each other, and I'd thought gawky Amber and her petite blonde mum were pretty mismatched too. But Tilda and her mother were like two different species. I bet Mrs Gilmore and her husband sometimes wondered if aliens from a distant galaxy swapped children in the night, taking away their pretty-in-pink cherub one day and leaving behind a princess of darkness.

"It's amazing that he wandered so far!" chatted Mrs Gilmore, bending over so we could help ourselves from the tray.

Of course, I had a new pet theory about that. I was pretty sure that Peaches hadn't so much rescued the rat as kidnapped him. Peaches seemed keen to send out signals that I should be friends with Tilda, and returning the wriggly rodent was one sure way of getting to know her better.

"It's such a relief to have him back!" Mrs Gilmore prattled on. "Well, not that Tilda's dad and I are exactly *fond* of him –"

Tilda tutted and rolled her eyes.

"– but our Tilly's missed him badly!"

"Tilly"? That sounded a bit too cute to suit Tilda Gilmore. I looked to check if TJ was grinning again. But he wasn't. I guess someone who hides the secret name of Titus isn't going to take the mick out of anyone else's name.

"Have you seen some of the photos she's taken of him?" said Mrs Gilmore, placing the tray on the carpet and pointing to a pinboard over the bookcase. "I keep saying she should send them into some of those nature documentaries! Don't I, Tilly?"

Tilda tutted and rolled her eyes again. Underneath her pale make-up I was sure there was a hint of a blush – though whether that was down to pride or embarrassment I wasn't sure.

"They look good," I said, getting to my feet and going over for a closer inspection.

Now *these* were more what you'd expect from Tilda; brooding black and white portraits that made Mr Noodles look like an extra from a vampire movie. And this one of a romantically overgrown garden with a grand gothic building looming... It was Joseph's house, looking totally different in the dusk light from the stark sunshine I always saw it bathed in.

"Oh!"

That startled squeak – that was me, catching

sight of the fat cat that purred on my bed every night. Only in this next photo of Tilda's he was fast asleep on an ornate, ivy-covered gravestone.

"It's Peaches!" I said out loud.

"You know him?" asked Tilda, getting up on her feet, still clutching Mr Noodles.

"He lives with me!" I told her. I couldn't say I "owned" him. Peaches was way too weirdly independent to be owned by anybody.

"I see him in the churchyard quite a lot," said Tilda. "That's his favourite place to sleep. Which is pretty amazing since that grave's the most interesting gravestone in there. It's—"

But I was way ahead of her. I'd already read the name carved on the stone.

"Elize Grainger. It's her grave," I muttered.

Another twist, another turn.

And this particular twist and turn ended up with the three of us standing staring at Elize's Grainger's grave, after scrambling through a tangle of untended ivy and holly bushes.

"Woof!" woofed Bob, from the safety of the path. With that long, furry coat he'd never have been able to follow me, TJ and Tilda through the snarls of hollybush prickles. As it was, Tilda had had to hoist up her tutu to save it from shredding.

132

Bob would have ended up coming out of it looking like he'd been attacked by a sheep-shearer who'd been sleepwalking.

"In one way, it's beautiful," Tilda was ruminating, tilting her head to one side as she read the inscription. "But it's a real shame that someone who's so important to this town has her gravestone hidden away in a corner like this."

"I'm going to tell that journalist girl," I said, sure that as soon as Jane heard about this, she'd have a photographer down and a campaign started to turn Elize Grainger's grave into a tidy beauty spot.

"'Spinster of this Parish…'" TJ read out a chunk of the inscription, holding back a curtain of ivy to do so. "'Spinster' is a rubbish word, isn't it? It makes it sound like she had a disease: 'Sorry, but your results show you're suffering from a severe case of spinsterisity.' Spinsterosis?"

While TJ rambled, I read over it again:

In remembrance of
Miss Elize Grainger,
spinster of this Parish.
Born 5th May 1830 in Barbados
Died 1st June 1930 in Portbay
Aged 100 years.
Her generosity and spirit will be much missed.

OK, so a trillion, gazillion people have died all over the world, for ever, and people die, who other people love, every day. But I suddenly felt a bundle of pangs: one for Elize, whose footsteps I'd felt I'd followed in, all the way from Sugar Bay to the den in Foxglove Cottage; one for my Nana Jones, who'd died before I was born, and didn't have a grave to visit since her ashes were scattered on a hillside; and one for my grandad Eddie, who might or might not be dead, but who was so unknown to me that it felt like he was.

And then of course there was the pang for Joseph ... who must have a gravestone somewhere too?

"That church in Somerton – I *bet* Joseph's buried there!" I said, excitedly. "I wish we could go there right now..."

("No *way*!" I could practically hear my parents gasp, causing an instant guilt-trip.)

"There's no place like home!" Mrs S-T's riddle wriggled its way inside my brain. (And here's a funny thing; I could practically hear "Somewhere Over the Rainbow" through the trees right now.

"Er, what's Bob doing?" TJ suddenly muttered, frowning over towards the gravel path.

What *was* Bob doing? He seemed to be watching someone strolling past, his hairy head following their every crunched step. He even leant forward when they were close enough, to have a typical doggy sniff of introduction.

Only there was nobody there.

"Wow..." murmured Tilda, her greeny-blue shadowed eyes glinting with the intrigue of it all.

TJ's face didn't look very excited; it looked sort of *grey*.

"Um, anybody else fancy doing a runner?" he suggested, in a fake, cheerful voice.

"Uh-huh," I nodded, very keen all of a sudden to get back to sunlight and daytrippers and hubbub.

Intrigued or not, Tilda didn't seem to be keen to be left behind, and hoisting up her tutu again, came charging out of the undergrowth and out of the graveyard with us...

Chapter 15

Being laughed at sucks

Sherbet: it's like fireworks on your tongue.

It doesn't matter how many times you have it, it still feels like a tingly, surprising zing when you taste it again.

And that's what it was like seeing the real live Megan again, instead of the text or e-mail version of her.

"STELLAAAAAAAA*AAAHHHHH*!!!!"

Her smile was practically all you could see as she stuck her head out of the train window.

Zing! went something in my tummy, as I waved madly back at her.

"Hiiiiiiiiiiiiiiiiiiiiiiiii!!!!!!!!!!!!!!!!" she bellowed, hurtling herself off the train (it had stopped, thank goodness) and running towards me along the platform in a blur of arms, legs, pink Adidas overnight bag and blonde bouncing ponytail.

When she hugged me, I could feel the soft velour of her dusky pink top brush softly against my arms, and her hair smelled of coconut shampoo. It was liked being bounded on by a scented Labrador puppy.

"Hello!" she said exuberantly to the rest of my waiting family, doling out warm hugs for them all, even though she didn't really know them too well.

"How ACE is this weekend going to be?!" She laughed, linking her arm into mine as we walked towards the car. "We are going to have SO much fun!"

"*And* we're going to have a sleepover tonight!" I let slip, though I'd originally planned on keeping that a surprise for later. (Mainly because my dad was still doing so-called "finishing touches" to my room today and I didn't want to set my heart on the sleepover till I knew it could definitely go ahead.)

"YAY!!" Megan shouted out, frightening the railway guard who was just about to wave the train off. Yep, Megan was so loud she could make a grown man jump; a grown man who didn't flinch a muscle when a fast train to London shot through the station at 100 mph...

And Megan chattered at about 100 mph, all the way down to the beach, where my parents dropped us off. Her chatting and laughing and goofing around – it all carried on as first TJ and

Bob joined us, and then Rachel came over from the direction of her mum's arty-crafty shop.

"See?! It's EASY!!" yelled Megan now. "Come on, Rach – *you* try!"

"I don't *want* to try," said Rachel, leaning back on her elbows in the sand and watching me and TJ muck about with Megan.

"Come on, surfer girl!" Megan dared her, grinning hard. Though the grin might have put Rachel off, since it was upside down.

"No – it's too *silly*!" groaned Rachel, slipping on her shades and trying to look cool.

"You don't have to do it like *me*," said Megan, starting to sound slightly out of breath, from walking backwards and forwards on her hands in an effort to keep her balance. "Just surf the normal way, like Stella and TJ!"

Me and TJ shot a quick look at each other and giggled, still trying to outdo each other on surfboard poses copied from all the lads doing their stuff on the waves.

"I don't want to surf upside-down like you, Megan," Rachel drawled, "and I don't want to surf 'normally', like Stella and TJ. 'Cause in case you haven't noticed, you aren't *really* surfing!"

"Aww…" grumbled Megan, flipping out of her handstand and landing on her feet, bum and hands on the warm Portbay sands. "You're NO fun, Rach!"

"And you're completely MAD, Megan!" said Rachel, a hint of a smile on her face.

TJ got off his surfboard (i.e. the outline of a surfboard that Megan had drawn in the sand for him) first.

"Rachel, you just didn't want to join in 'cause you were scared that some of the surfer lads would spot you mucking around. *And* 'cause your big brother and all his mates are over there too."

I think TJ was trying to show Rach up; make her feel shallow for not getting up on the empty fourth surfboard that Megan had drawn in the sand using a stick that Bob had padded down to the beach with today. I was happy to have fooled around doing surfer impressions, and hoped some of the surfers really *had* seen me and got an idea of how truly stupid and show-offy they looked.

"You know something?" said Rachel, dipping her sunglasses down on her nose a little and eyeballing him. "You are *exactly* right, TJ O'Connell."

Well, there was no arguing with that. And there was no arguing with the fact that Megan's infectious silliness was like a breath of fluffy fresh air after the dark fascination of yesterday's spooky visits to Tilda's house and then the churchyard...

And since none of us were arguing with Rachel, she gave a triumphant smile and lay back down to sunbathe. Pity no one told Bob it was her moment of triumph; if they had, he might have moved over a fraction so that when he started to power-dig in the sand for the doggy fun of it, he didn't shower Rachel with sand at the same time.

"Yeuchhh! Get him to *stop*!!" shrieked Rachel, sitting bolt upright, pulling a horrified face and trying to shield her face from yet more sand showers with her arms.

A couple of the waiting surfer boys down by the shingle turned round to see what the fuss was about, same as Si Riley and his mates. Maybe it was just as well that Rachel was temporarily blinded or she'd have been mortified at the attention her mini-drama had attracted.

Actually, it was when I glanced over at Si and his crew that I noticed *another* mini-drama unfolding. As Si's boy mates snickered in our direction, Tilda Gilmore seemed to spot her tiny window of opportunity to get Si Riley's reluctant attention. I saw her reach over and put her hand gently on his shoulder, her dark-lipsticked mouth talking, her pale face and huge, kohl-rimmed eyes pleading.

From our patch of beach, we were too far away to hear normal speech, never mind whispered, beseeching words, but I could see the scene unfolding, like a snatch of some old silent movie reel.

At Tilda's unwelcome touch and questioning, an embarrassed Si tried to shake her off with a physical and a verbal shrug. Which of course got his easy-to-entertain cronies spinning their long-haired, beanie-wearing heads around. They might not have understood what exactly had brought their leader (Si) to this point with Tilda (the just-tolerated screwball), but for all of them it seemed worthy of a cruel laugh.

"What's up with Tilda?" I heard TJ suddenly ask, spotting an ashen-faced Tilda struggle to her feet in the shifting sands, and try to leave the baying group with her dignity and tutu intact.

"I think Rachel's brother has just tried to give her a subtle hint that he doesn't fancy her, but in a really *unsubtle* way..." I muttered, spotting Tilda suddenly fix her tragic, Manga-styled eyes on me, like I was her life raft in a sea of shame.

"*Who* are you talking about?" asked a disorientated Rachel, trying to rub the last of the sand off her face with her towel, and giving herself an unexpected exfoliation at the same time.

"Tilda Wotsit," answered Megan, sitting up on her haunches like a meerkat.

"Don't ... don't stare at her too much. She must be having a bad time," I said, imagining how the fiercely independent but horribly-in-love Tilda must be feeling right now. (Fiercely embarrassed and horribly mortified, perhaps?)

"Sorry, won't stare..." mumbled Megan, remembering the background I'd told her about Tilda by e-mail all this week. "I'm going to go."

"Go where?" I asked, confused. Megan had only been back in Portbay for forty-five minutes.

"Go ask those guys if I can have a turn!" she said fearlessly, heading off towards the surfers in her blue T-shirt, pink bikini bottoms and a "they-can-only-knock-me-back" wave of her hands.

How could she do that? I guess Megan didn't know yet that they'd taken over the beach and been overheard moaning about the facilities, and were generally not making any mates around Portbay.

"Tilda isn't *really* coming over here, is she?" Rachel growled low, watching warily as Megan's skinny, muscly legs stomped one way while Tilda's stripy legs strode closer and closer to us.

"Why not?" I asked her, sorry to see the intolerant version of Rachel emerging, especially after me and TJ had just finished telling her about our encounter with Tilda yesterday; about giving her back Mr Noodles; about the photo of Peaches on the gravestone; about going to the churchyard and finding Elize's grave; about us hurrying away when we all got spooked. (Though being spooked obviously gave Tilda a thrill, judging by the big grin on her face and the fact that she'd muttered "Excellent!" before regaining her composure and heading back home to her not-very-long-lost rat.)

"'Cause I'm not really up for a bit of chit-chat with a witch," Rachel grumbled. "Or someone who makes up mad coded messages that freak out my brother..."

"Don't be silly," I grumbled back, knowing I didn't have time to say any more than that before Tilda was upon us.

"Hey," said Tilda, to nobody in particular, flopping down beside us in a puff of sand.

"Hi," I said back.

I thought about adding: "How's things?" or "What're you up to?", but the answers would have been "Terrible" and "Just busy being humiliated", so I didn't bother.

"Um, hi, guys!" a voice called down from the prom just above us.

It was Amber, leaning on the blue railings and

beaming a wary smile our way.

Tilda froze, like a human goth statue. If she did that up on the prom, she could earn a fortune from the holidaymakers.

"Stella, you're into Joseph's house, right?" said Tilda urgently, now standing up and brushing sand off her tutu.

It didn't seem likely that she was in the mood to get to know Amber right now.

"Er, yes ... of course," I muttered, exchanging a quick glance with Amber. She gave me a well-I-tried shrug back.

"Well, they're taking the chandelier out this morning. Want to go take a look?" asked Tilda.

From her body language, she was trying to act casual and in control, but her eyes were twinkling with tears.

"Uh..."

I *couldn't* go with her. I wanted to; I mean, I wanted to see what was going on over in Sugar Bay and I sort of wanted to help Tilda too. But Megan had only just arrived...

OK, all that was what the sensible, *left*-hand side of my brain said.

The more intuitive, what-the-heck *right*-hand side of my brain said out loud: "I'll just go and have a look and come straight back. I'll be twenty minutes. Can you look after Megan?"

"She's kind of looking after herself." TJ laughed, nodding over to where Megan was getting a lesson on how to stand on a real board (the right way up) from two bemused-by-her-cheek surfers (the big, muscly doughballs).

As I hurried after an already stomping Tilda, I could feel Rachel's incredulous look boring into my back...

Boy, could Tilda walk fast.

I was out of breath as I trailed two footsteps behind her in my flip-flops along to the far, far end of the prom, where a set of uneven steps cut into rock led up to the caravan park on the headland.

I was panting even more a few minutes later, after we'd climbed the steps, weaved between the boxy holiday homes, and found ourselves a large rock to sit on.

From here I could see the flurry of activity going on at the house below, and something unexpected – a whole bunch of the surfer boys had found their way to Sugar Bay and were zapping around in a sea free of swimmers, paddlers and dogs snapping at the white horses. I'd *wondered* why fewer of them were posing around Portbay the last day or two. Suddenly, I felt a wave-sized ripple of anger, thinking that the dopey surfer dudes and their large egos (and surfboards) had invaded *my* special, secret place…

Stop it, a sensible part of my brain said sternly. *You have hardly any time left to enjoy this place. Think of the good stuff!*

And so I concentrated on thinking of the good stuff; I thought that from this viewpoint, I could just about imagine where Elize Grainger had positioned herself, to draw that view of the house on the card she'd sent to Joseph's granddaughter, Violet.

"They're going to have to take the chandelier to bits, to move it all by hand up the hill," said Tilda, nodding first at the men coming out with wrapped bundles of canvas from the house, and then inclining her head towards the lorry parked close to us, close to the top of the scree path that led down to Sugar Bay.

"I can't stay long," I wheezed, wishing my chest would stop pounding. "Our friend Megan just got here today – she's only here for the weekend."

"Sorry to drag you away," mumbled Tilda. "I just didn't want to be at the beach any more. Getting laughed at sucks."

"Who was, uh, laughing at you?" I asked, deciding that acting innocent was the least embarrassing option for Tilda.

"Si Riley's mates."

"Well, they're *your* mates too, aren't they?"

"Not really," said Tilda, scrunching up her nose, at the same time picking moss off the rock with her bitten, purple-painted thumbnail. "I know they only put up with me 'cause of him. But I don't think he wants to know me any more either…"

"Why not?"

Is pretending not to know something a kind of a lie? My cheeks seemed to think so from the way they were flushing.

"I dunno. I thought we had stuff in common. Both being the town freaks. Freak One and Freak Two…"

Tilda smiled a wry smile as she said the last bit.

"Freak what?" I asked, a little lost.

"We kind of nicknamed each other Freak One and Freak Two. We used to write these funny messages to each other, sign 'em as F1 and F2, so they were just our little secret."

Ah … so the last mystery of the mysterious coded message clunked into place.

"And *she's* probably laughing at me right now," Tilda suddenly burst out, her face clouding over before I got the chance to think of something pacifying to say about Tilda's Freak One going cold on her.

"She who?"

"That Amber from the café," Tilda muttered darkly. "She's *dying* to get her claws into him."

"Oh, *no*! That's absolutely *not* true!" I burst out. "Amber's not into him *that* way!"

"She looked pretty pleased with herself yesterday morning in the café, when he was hugging her!"

Urgh… How could I explain that away, without telling her that Si was actually using Amber as a human shield to hide behind? A white lie, quick, please…

"But I was right there – he wasn't *hugging* her … he was trying to point out a couple of surfers at sea, and Amber couldn't make them out. So he just grabbed her by the waist and moved her till she could see them!"

Tilda looked like she wasn't too convinced by my lie – but really wanted to be.

"He went to a wedding with her last weekend, didn't he?"

"Yeah … but that's because Rachel sort of blackmailed him into it!" I admitted. "But Si and Amber ended up getting on OK, just 'cause they're both mad on *Twilight*!"

"I hate *Twilight*. How come everyone's so into it?"

She might have been ranting about some dumb, cult movie, but I could see that wave of relief visible on Tilda's face. OK, so she hadn't admitted outright to being mad about Si, but if I could just get her to stop resenting Amber, then that would be something. Specially since they were in the same year at school. Specially since neither of them had any good friends in their year. I mean, if I could get Amber and Tilda talking, *really* talking, then this time next week, they could be hanging out together, if they ended up in the same classes.

Fat chance of it happening anytime soon, though.

Unless, of course…

"Hey, Tilda," I said, knowing I was about to come out with something I might regret.

"Uh-huh?"

"Are you doing anything tonight?"

Depending on your viewpoint, it was a brilliant/stupid, inspired/deranged idea, but all that was running through my head right now was one question: I wonder what goth ballerinas wear to sleepovers…?

Chapter 16

She wouldn't. (Would she?)

If you didn't look too closely, my room looked great.

But like any house makeover programme on TV, it had been a mad rush to get it finished, before my sleepover guests arrived. There hadn't been time to put up shelves or pictures, and a tacky patch of paint above the door hadn't quite dried yet, but as Megan said, no one would notice any of that if we had enough crisps and nibbles to distract them.

Megan had been brilliant. She'd cheerfully helped lug the chest of drawers and mattress back into my room, even though she was limping after landing on a rock due to her first attempt at surfing. (How nice of the self-obsessed surf guys to look out for her, I *don't* think.) Then she'd even gone and got a scented candle from my mum ("burning it'll help kill the paint fumes").

While Dad had been temporarily screwing my

undipped bedroom door back in place, and I'd been wrestling my newly washed white duvet cover on, Megan had even nipped out into the garden and picked a bunch of mismatching wild flowers to stick in a vase on my window sill.

"I like the colour of the walls," said Rachel, as she unfurled her sleeping bag.

"Peppermint!" said Megan, as she plumped up the airbed with a whistling foot pump.

"Apple green," I corrected her.

It wasn't till I'd walked in this afternoon and seen my bedroom all finished(ish) that I'd realized the pale, apple green was the exact shade of Mrs Sticky Toffee's raincoat. I'd actually chosen it because the white muslin drapes Mum had ordered for my windows had tiny dots the same colour, along with meringue pink and sky blue dots too.

"It all looks brilliant!" said Amber, her long legs curled underneath her as she sat on my now re-erected bed.

I was glad all my friends had nice things to say. And I was also glad that the patched-up single airbed, and the double one we'd borrowed from our neighbour Margaret, covered so much of the floor that you couldn't really see that it was still just bare boards, with a faint outline of white where Dad had spilled the gloss paint and not cleaned it up very well.

Practically invisible as it was, the floor still worried me; the last thing I wanted was for a rogue splinter to cause a puncture in the middle of the night. And speaking of punctures, I'd have to remember to close the bedroom door so that Peaches and his claws couldn't get in…

"Hey, tonight, are we going to have to talk about nail varnish and boy bands and bras and stuff?" asked TJ.

"Shut up, you idiot!" Rachel told him, rolling her eyes.

Yep, for tonight only, TJ was an honorary girl, allowed to laze around with us in pyjamas and eat and talk rubbish till late – when he'd have to go through to my brothers' room and sleep on the sunlounger Dad had stuck in there for him.

So far, TJ had taken his honorary girl status very seriously (I don't think), turning up at my front door with a badge he'd got at a car boot sale saying "Girl Power", and his floppy brown hair gathered up into two tiny nubbins of bunches.

"By the way, *please* tell me you only put those in as you got here," I said, nodding at his bunches, held in place with two Angelina Ballerina hair bobbles borrowed from Ellie.

"Yeah, like I'd *really* wander the streets looking like this, waiting for people to shout 'Freak!' at me!"

"Well, being called a freak doesn't seem to bother Tilda Gilmore." Rachel shrugged. "I thought you were maybe going for the more extreme look, now you and Stella are so *matey* with her!"

Gulp.

The very mention of Tilda's name made me feel sick in the same way as when you know the teacher's about to ask you for your homework and you're about to admit you forgot to do it.

"*I'm* not that matey with her!" TJ protested. "I mean, she looks pretty amazing in a bizarre kind of way, but she's also amazingly … *bizarre*. Like those coded, stalkery messages to your brother, Rach. No *wonder* he's trying to hide away from her."

"Yeah. Then hide away behind *Amber*!" Rachel giggled, remembering yesterday's tales from the Hot Pepper Jelly, when Amber was used like a tall, skinny, red-headed shield. "But whatever... *Stella's* still her new mate, aren't you?"

I couldn't quite think of a way to answer Rachel – she'd had to leave and go help her mum out in the Portbay Galleria by the time I got back from the headland today.

"It's more like… Y'know…" I mumbled, wriggling on the airbed so much that it made unpleasant farting noises.

What I knew for *sure* was that I was a coward.

A complete coward, who couldn't admit to Rachel, and Amber and Megan and TJ, that I'd invited someone else to our sleepover.

The way I justified it to myself was that Tilda hadn't sounded too keen when I asked her, or at least she hadn't said, "That would be lovely – yes please". In fact, she'd only muttered, "Oh," when I suggested it, and "Thanks," when I'd scribbled down my address before leaving her sitting on the rock, watching the chandelier get dismantled and packed up.

Maybe Tilda wasn't keen because she thought that we really *would* be talking about nail varnish, boy bands and bras, or maybe it was because she couldn't think of anything more awful than being stuck in a room all night with girls who she either didn't know very well or didn't much like in the first place.

So Tilda wouldn't come. No *way*. Absolutely not. She'd probably be holed up in her black room right now, writing gloomy poetry about love and feeding Mr Noodles pumpkin seeds.

(Bing-bong! went the doorbell downstairs.)

"So what happens with sleepovers? Do we get changed into our pyjamas now?" asked Amber.

(She'd no idea that my stomach had just tied itself in a double bow knot at the sound of the bell.)

"Yeah! Do you like mine? I bought them specially," said Rachel, pulling out a pair of loose, red, hip-hugging bottoms and a white vest top with a patchwork velvet heart on the front.

(I could hear muffled voices downstairs as one of my parents answered the door.)

"These are cute, aren't they?" Megan laughed, holding up a T-shirt and short set with little Scottie dogs scampering all over them.

(I was *sure* I could hear footsteps on the stairs.)

"*I've* only got my old checked PJs with me," Amber said apologetically, as if she was suddenly worried that tonight was going to turn into a nightwear fashion show.

(I was imagining the footsteps on the stairs, I was sure I was.)

"Well, here's mine!" said TJ, kicking off his trainers and standing, arms outstretched, in the grey T-shirt and baggy cotton shorts he'd arrived in.

"Boys are *so* scuzzy," Rachel droned at him in disgust.

"Ah, but I'm a girl, remember?" said TJ, pointing to his bunches. "We're just *five* girlies hanging out…"

"Six, I think!" said Mum, from the doorway of my room. She was smiling warmly, but still managed to throw me the briefest of quizzical looks. I couldn't blame her; it wasn't like I'd actually *told* her to expect a new friend in a tutu and leather jacket.

(Oops.)

"I brought Xenon – hope that's OK," Tilda said defensively, her flower-decorated boots staying on the landing side of the doorway, as if she was waiting for the signal to come in.

"Um, yeah! S-s-sure! Come in!!" I heard myself babble, my old-time stammer returning due to self-inflicted stress.

I didn't dare look round at everyone else's faces. Mum and Tilda were probably getting a great view of five very different expressions that read as various versions of "Huh?!?"

"Thanks," said Tilda, stomping into the room, and flopping down on to the hard floor with her largish rucksack, and wearing her rat like a small browny-grey scarf. "I brought some stuff. Is that OK?"

Quickly flipping open the catches of her

rucksack, Tilda pulled out a tightly rolled-up sleeping bag, a huge bag of marshmallows, a bag of skinny long sticks, some black pyjamas (where do you buy black pyjamas?), a book, two tiny ceramic bowls and a small see-through bag filled with something dubious.

"Rat food," she said quickly, seeing me staring. "I just need some water in the other bowl, and Xenon will be fine."

"I'll get that for you," said Mum, leaning over and taking one of the bowls. "And I'll get Stella's dad to bring up some cushions off the sofa for you to use as a bed ... er..."

"T-T-Tilda," I jumped in.

"Tilda ... right." Mum nodded, before retreating.

I had to hand it to Tilda, it was pretty brave of her to come tonight. Or she was just pretty desperately in need of new friends. When your only true friend is a boy who's now rejecting you, it's not much fun. I just wished *this* could've seemed like more fun to her. The stunned silence must have made her want to pack up her bag and run right out again. If only my panic-stricken brain could think of something non-stammering to say...

"Well, will we all get changed?" Megan said so

breezily that I could've kissed her.

"TJ needs to get lost first," growled Rachel, sounding like a very grumpy Siamese cat. Though she was obviously less grumpy with TJ being there than this strange cuckoo of a girl.

"Don't worry, I'm getting lost," said TJ, leaning unnecessarily on my shoulder as he headed for the door (except I guess it was necessary; necessary for him to give me a quick "What's going on?" squeeze as he went by).

Those few minutes it took us five girls to get changed were the most awkward few minutes of my life. No one looked at each other, and no one talked. We just kept our heads down and wriggled and unbuttoned and unzipped in a blur until one by one, we all became still and slowly gazed up to see ourselves transformed into our night-time selves.

"You look naked without your tutu!" Megan announced, grinning Tilda's way.

Tilda was still in her full make-up – I wondered if she'd take it off before she went to sleep, or keep it on and risk looking like a portrait that had been left out in the rain all night – all smudged and stained.

"I'm Megan, by the way. And do you know Rachel and Amber?"

God bless Megan, for wading right in there in the middle of this embarrassment.

"Mmm, kind of," muttered Tilda, repetitively stroking her wriggly rat.

I half expected to see Rachel shooting me daggers, but instead, she was busy flattening herself against the chest of drawers and staring at Xenon as if the rat was a small, unexploded bomb.

"Um … what're the sticks for, Tilda?"

Amber – what a star. She was trying to make chit-chat, despite the fact that she was probably worried that this could be the most uncomfortable night of her life. I couldn't have blamed her if she hated me for inviting Tilda without telling her, but I really hoped she wouldn't…

"They're skewers. Got a candle?" asked Tilda.

"Yep!" said Megan, reaching over and grabbing the scented candle and kitchen matches she'd laid on top of the chest of drawers.

"Well, if we make a space in the middle of the floor, we can light the candle, put the skewers in the marshmallows and toast them."

"ACE!" cooed Megan.

"Yum!" said Amber.

"Really?" I said dubiously, wondering if the marshmallows would end up magnolia-flavoured, since that was what the scented candle was supposed to smell of.

Rachel said nothing – she was just rigid with horrified fascination as Xenon wriggled and ran down the length of Tilda's neck and arms and back again.

Megan immediately made herself marsh-mallow monitor, lighting the candle, then sticking skewer sticks into marshmallows and doling them out.

"And I brought this – thought it could be fun…"

Tilda held up the book that had tumbled out of her rucksack: *Spells for Teenage Witches*.

"What sort of stuff's in there?" I asked, panicking slightly that any minute now Tilda was going to insist on the ritual slaughter of some unknown small animals in her bag or something. Where do you get books called *Spells for Teenage Witches*, anyway? Maybe Tilda got it from her mentor, Madame Xara, the psychic on the prom. Maybe that's what she'd been in collecting from her earlier in the week?

"Hold on – here's the contents page," said Tilda. "There're spells we could try like … like the 'Good Fortune' spell, or the 'Rainbow Peace' spell, or the 'Notice Me' spell."

Suddenly, I didn't feel so wary of Tilda. If she

was a *true* witch, she'd have done her "Notice Me" spell on Si Riley ages ago, and Freak One and Freak Two would be strolling into the sunset at the beach, madly in love by now. I took a second to sneak a quick peek at my other girlfriends. Whether Tilda was a bona fide witch or not (probably not), I was relieved to see that they all looked instantly perky. Funny how a spooky spell book can break the ice, just like that. (Was there a "Breaking the Ice" spell inside?)

"Um, that spell about getting someone to notice you," came a voice from the other side of the door. "D'you think I could maybe try it out on me?"

"Aw, TJ!" I said with a smile, opening the door so he could step his way in, over all the squashy beds. "Did you think we'd forgotten about you?!"

"Well, it's easy to forget things, eh, Stella?" TJ said with a cheeky wink.

To forget things like mentioning I'd invited Tilda tonight, he meant...

"There!" murmured Megan, holding up the first, slightly burnt, slightly melty marshmallow.

"Mmm, nice!" bellowed TJ, reaching forward, grabbing it off the skewer and sticking it in his mouth.

"TJ!"

There was a sudden flurry of pretend outrage and shock from all of us at TJ's thieving ways, while we all jostled to toast our own next.

"Come on, then – read out one of the spells!" Rachel challenged Tilda.

I didn't care if Rachel was challenging her – at least it meant she was *talking* to Tilda.

"OK," nodded Tilda, getting stuck into the book again. "Maybe—"

"Maybe there's one about how to get my brother to fancy you?"

Oooh...

Ouch...

Nooooooo...

That was *so* below-the-belt that I couldn't *believe* Rachel had said it. But then she probably couldn't believe I'd invited Tilda along tonight.

Tilda's face changed from hurt to furious to vulnerable to unreadable, with the minutest of muscle spasms. She was going to walk, I was sure.

"You might always get what you want, Rachel," said Tilda finally, her voice quivering only very slightly. "But the rest of us lesser beings don't always – spell books or no spell books."

Rachel didn't seem to know what to say to that. None of us did – except TJ.

"Hey, girls, when I said I'd come to a girly

sleepover I wasn't expecting a full-on cat fight!" he said lightly, breaking the silence.

Then Megan chipped in. "C'mon, let's try *some* proper spells now!" she said breezily, attempting to gloss over the awkwardness fast.

Tilda was very still for a second, her greeny-blue eyelids dropped down towards the book in her hand as she considered whether to get up and go, or stay and brave it out.

"This one's called the 'Good Fortune' spell," she suddenly came out with. "And for this, we're supposed to get some stuff together."

I felt strangly proud of Tilda for brazening it out.

"What sort of stuff? Like a broomstick and a fake, warty nose?" TJ grinned, joining in with the brazening.

"*No*," said Tilda, with a shake of her bob, and a slight smile playing at her dark red lips. "It says here that we need a crystal, an egg cup, a small bowl and some rainwater…"

"Well, *first*, we might need a 'Find A Cloud' spell, so we can get some rain!" TJ pointed out, looking out of my wide-open bedroom window, at the warm, late summer night outside.

We all found ourselves forgetting the awkwardness and giggling a little at that, except for Tilda … at least for a second or two, till she realized we weren't laughing *at* her. And a sheepish-looking Rachel eventually joined in too – maybe she'd gotten over the fact that Tilda's crush was on *her* brother, and realized she was just a girl with a crush. Or maybe she just realized that if she was going to have any fun tonight she was going to have to at least pretend she'd gotten over it…

"Like I said, I've only just got this book – I haven't read through it properly yet." Tilda shrugged, her face relaxing into a wide smile.

"Try another one!" Megan encouraged her, looking like a contented hamster with two cheeks stuffed full of toasted marshmallows.

"Um … how about…"

There was no sound except hushed breaths and the snap of paper as Tilda flicked through pages.

"Meeeeooooooowwwwww!"

CRASHHHHH!

The six of us practically levitated in shock. The sound – a terrible yeowl and a splinter of glass breaking – had come from the window.

"Peaches?!" I frowned, spotting that my larger-than-life cat had leapt up from the kitchen roof, on to my window sill, clumsily knocking over the vase of wild flowers that Megan had left there. Peaches ignored my stern tone and stared hard at something in the middle of the room.

Uh-oh…

"Omigod!" Tilda cried out, grabbing an open can of Tango near me and aiming its contents straight at Rachel.

"What are you *doing?*" Rachel shrieked, catching sight of the arc of fizziness heading her way.

What she *hadn't* seen, not till the last second, were the beads of fire that were burning through the wooden skewer she was carelessly holding too far into the candle flame.

Sploosh…!

"Here," TJ said gently, taking the juice-dampened, blackened wood skewer from a shocked Rachel's hand.

"Here," said Amber, passing a box of tissues to Rachel so that she could pat her Tango'd pyjamas off.

"Maybe I'll ask your mum for a bowl for these," said Megan, picking up the bag of marshmallows.

"Clever puss!" muttered Tilda, stroking Peaches as he slithered and weaved his way between the makeshift beds.

"Yes, he is…" I said, reaching out for a cuddle too, since I knew as well as Tilda did that Peaches wasn't just a fat cat who'd knocked something over; his emerald eyes had seen the accident waiting to happen.

For a stunned moment, we were all quiet; a little bit spooked and shocked and serious (and in Rachel's case, *damp*).

"Hey, nothing BAD happened!" Megan finally announced. "I mean, yeah, it *nearly* did, but it didn't! So why don't we do something fun?"

"Like?" Rachel muttered darkly, as if she was expecting Megan to suggest a water pistol fight.

"I dunno... Like see who can do a headstand the longest!"

We all winced. The winner would be Megan, since we'd played that game before at the beach and knew that every one of us – except Megan – tended to last less than five seconds.

"How about a game? Do you have Monopoly or something, Stella?" Amber asked.

"I *did*, but Jake and Jamie dropped all the pieces and half the money into the drain at the side of the house."

"We could tell jokes!" TJ grinned.

"You *are* a joke." Megan giggled, leaning over and flicking one of his bunches.

"Well ... we could always tell ghost stories."

A breathy chorus of "yeah!"s rumbled around the room at Tilda's suggestion. Even Rachel seemed to look vaguely intrigued.

Everyone's eyes fixed on her, sure as I was that Tilda Gilmore would not only have an excellent back catalogue of ghost stories, but that she'd be the best storyteller too.

"Amber, can you turn off that light beside you so it's more atmospheric?" asked Tilda, getting settled and ready to scare the pyjamas off us.

Also getting settled was Peaches, curling himself into a fat, purring ball on my lap. He looked like a furry Buddha, smiling serenely around at us all, one animated girl talking and five rapt faces listening.

I had a feeling that Tilda – despite the coded desperation, the pet rat and the awkwardness with Rachel – might be on her way to being one of us now…

Chapter 17

Guided tours and uninvited invitations. . .

"The hand crawling along the floor, trailing blood ... *that* was the worst one!" said Amber, from somewhere in the middle of the Foxglove Cottage crop circle.

"No – it was the one about the face LOOMING out of the lake, *definitely*!" I heard Megan say next.

"Wait – you think *those* were worse than the one about the girl seeing her dead boyfriend's handwriting appear on the steamy bathroom mirror?!" gasped Rachel disbelievingly.

Last night, we'd all got spooked, swapped stories, talked rubbish, even sung (in hushed voices, after Mum came through and moaned – not to mention TJ, who felt that singing was one girly step too far), till late, late, late, or early, early, early, depending on how you wanted to look at it.

But it didn't matter, since the two most important things were that...

a) After a night of bonding, all my friends had

seemed to get into the girl behind the obsessional crush on Si – even Rachel, once she'd got over the fact that Tilda had slapped back her sarky remarks (and saved her from setting my room on fire).

b) No one had to get up at the crack of dawn – even Amber had arranged to start her shift in the Hot Pepper Jelly at lunchtime.

It's just a shame that two small boys didn't see it that way.

They started beating up TJ with thrown toys at 5.45 a.m. and after trying to ignore them and use his pillow as a shield for as long as possible, TJ had had to give up when Jake managed to undo the top of his former bedtime bottle and empty warm, smelly milk over TJ's chest.

TJ had tried very hard to be quiet when he tiptoed into my room, looking for his bag with a clean T-shirt in it. But tiptoeing on inflatable beds is like trying to ride a bike in a bouncy castle – it's going to end *badly*.

In fact, TJ managed to tip over at such an angle that he squashed a little bit of everyone who was sleeping on the floor, except – thankfully – Xenon, who was curled up snoozling in the safety of Megan's left trainer.

After that rude awakening, it was a case of *more* yakking, flicking through magazines, putting on make-up (Tilda), taking turns showering and finally getting dressed, by which time we all stumbled out into the bright morning sunshine.

Breakfast (a mound of toast, with jars of peanut butter and jam, plus two cartons of orange juice) was being served in the corn circle. Amber, Rachel and Megan were the only ones diving into it at the moment, 'cause TJ was over by the back door where the phone reception was better, checking in with his mum to see how lonely old Bob had coped without him.

As for me and Tilda, well, I was just to about to give her a guided tour.

"This is it," I said, opening the door of the outhouse and ushering her into my tiny but cosy den. (In the space of half a second, I spotted the since-decoded message on my desk, plus aflabet, and hurriedly shoved them in the top drawer.)

"Wow ... I'd absolutely *love* to have something like this!" murmured Tilda, glancing around at the desk and table at the window, at the comfy chair in the corner, at the shells and driftwood and photos and trinkets on the shelves, at the board where my fifty pound cheque was pinned, along with the photo of Granny Jones and Grandad Eddie, the old newspaper cutting about Elize that I'd forgotten to hand into the museum, and my most recent artistic doodle, which happened to be…

Urgh.

I wasn't exactly the most confident person in the world, but normally I was fine with letting people see my artwork, since I knew it wasn't bad. Not award-winning stuff, but not rotten, by a long way.

Still, this … my latest ninja fairy, with her stripy tights, tutu and chunky boots. If Tilda didn't recognize herself in that then she'd have to be registered clinically blind. I wished I'd managed to shove *that* out of sight in my top drawer too…

"Nice!" she said, and laughed softly, sensing my embarrassment. "Is she a fairy that can make wishes come true?"

"Probably not," I said, thinking that the one wish I most wanted at the moment was for Tilda not to have seen this.

"No, probably not…" Tilda repeated wistfully.

I guess *her* one wish had something to do with Si Riley, and as she'd let on last night, she knew as well as anyone that it had fat chance of coming true.

"Are these your grandparents?" she asked, sounding brighter, as she pointed at the black-and-white fairground snap.

"Uh-huh." I nodded. "Though I've never met either of them. They split up before my grandad Eddie even knew he was going to be, well, a *dad*, never mind a grandad. And my mum's mum – that's Granny Jones – she died before I was born."

"That's a shame… You look like a real mixture of the two of them."

It felt strange to think I was nothing like my mum and dad and brothers, but some genetic throwback to people I'd never known. A bit like the strange friendship I felt for Elize and Joseph, though they lived for-ever-and-a-bit ago.

"And what's this?" asked Tilda, pointing to the yellowed, much-treasured newspaper clipping.

"It's from 1930 – it's all about Elize Grainger celebrating her hundredth birthday, right here. My house used to belong to her, and this den was her art studio!"

Tilda peered at the grainy photo of Elize, posed in the garden with her easel, and a table with a rose-patterned teacup on it by her side.

"I can't believe it…" she murmured.

"Neither can I. It's so spooky that she ended up here!"

"I don't mean *that*; I mean *this*!" said Tilda, pointing her bitten-to-the-quick fingernail at a *something* near Elize's feet. "Remind you of anyone?"

I'd never spotted the blob by Miss Grainger's dainty shoes before. Maybe I'd just thought it was a loosely circular blur of grass, caused by old-fashioned photography. But on closer inspection, it wasn't.

"It looks kind of like –"

"– Peaches!" Tilda laughed, as our eyes sought out his features, like one of those two-in-one trick drawings where you see a bearded guy one way round and a prim lady in an Edwardian dress the other way.

But I had exactly one-quarter of a nanosecond to absorb what I was *maybe* seeing before Rachel started yelling for us to come out, sharpish.

"What?" I called to her, wading through the overgrown grasses to the communal crop circle.

"Amber's just had a text…" said Rachel, slowing down when she saw Tilda re-enter the circle. "From … from my brother."

"Oh. What's *that* about, then?" I asked Amber, trying to put on a fake cheerful expression, knowing how much those few words could destroy Tilda.

"He's … um … just reminding me about that party that's happening tonight at Sugar Bay," said Amber, trying to act relaxed too, but making every word sound staged and awkward.

I'd forgotten about that. Since he'd mentioned it in the café yesterday morning, so much had happened that I hadn't had a chance to process that piece of information.

"Yeah, nice, huh? Si is *such* a waste of space that he didn't even think to tell *me* about it!" growled Rachel, thinking about her own feelings and forgetting about Tilda's in the meantime.

As for Tilda, she flopped down, deflated and cross-legged on to the ground. I think she knew what me and all my friends probably suspected already; that there *wouldn't* be a similar invite left on Tilda's phone either.

But forgetting Rachel and Tilda's similar-but-different-hurt feelings for a moment... What about mine? How could people who didn't care enough to visit Sugar Bay and Joseph's house on a regular basis consider they had a right to hold a party there, in such a rare, special place?

"Are you going to go?" I asked a pink-cheeked, awkward-looking Amber.

"I – I –"

"*Course* you should! It sounds good!" I heard Tilda suddenly say mock-cheerfully, though she was talking directly to her knees at the time, which kind of gave away the fact that her heart was well and truly and horribly broken.

Amber looked uncomfortable for a moment, but then she spoke again.

"Yes, it *should* be good," she said, starting to text back a reply to Si Riley.

"What are you saying exactly?" asked Megan, leaning over to peek at Amber's screen.

"I'm saying I'll definitely be there," said Amber, her eyes fixed to the keypad as she texted her response.

"But what about *us*?" asked TJ, trying to stride into the crop circle on his shorter-than-average legs. I hadn't realized he'd even caught part of this conversation.

"There's nothing in his message about me coming on my own," Amber said, and shrugged.

And of *course* she wasn't going to come on her own.

There'd be a gang of five uninvited guests trailing her.

"Plus *Bob*, of course," said TJ as if he was reading my mind…

Chapter 18

Amber's own, personal gatecrashers

Frankie was practically *purple* with jealousy, I could tell, even by text.

U R going 2 a party? On a beach? With Rachel's brother and his mates? How cool is that?! Not fair – my Saturday night is having tea with my gran... Wanna swap?

No thanks, I texted back as I got ready to go out.

By ready, I didn't mean anything too dramatic. The whole afternoon, me and my friends had ummed and ahhed, talking about what to wear, and finally decided to look just like our normal selves, since we hadn't a *clue* what you were meant to wear to a beach party. (Surf shorts? Hula grass skirts? A ballgown and flippers?) Looking like our normal selves was also the best option, considering that Megan only had an identical change of tracksuit with her, Amber was going to be coming to mine straight from work, and TJ said there was no way he was willing to dress up for anything, unless someone wanted to bribe him with a big bag of money and a PlayStation 2 with a dumper-truckload of games to go with it.

As no one *did* turn up with a big bag of money, a PlayStation 2 and a dumper-truckload of games, TJ was now sitting on one of our sofas, wearing his oldest, worn combats and his favourite "I'm with Stupid" T-shirt. Speaking of stupid, Bob was lying panting on the rug, oblivious to the glitter gel that Rachel had combed on to the tips of his ears, *and* to the fact that my brothers were dropping piles of popcorn on to his fur.

"Ooh!" Mum and Dad oohed, as us five girls did a turn for them in the living room.

OK, so it wasn't as if they were blown away by the sight of our mixture of T-shirts, denim skirts and jeans – it was more Rachel's finishing touches. Rachel – who'd put her foot down and insisted on doing a *little* party styling. She'd come along today with a giant make-up bag packed with straighteners, curling irons, hair clips and face-and-body-glitter, and got to work on us all – minus TJ, of course.

Rachel was first for a twirl, with her long, dark hair ferociously straightened and her nails twinkling with silver-glittered varnish. Megan was next, with a blue streak of glitter in her blonde hair, which had been set free from her ponytail and flicked up at the bottom. Amber – with red ringlets and copper glitter sweeping at the corners of her eyes – gave the shyest, quickest spin you'd ever seen. Then it was *my* turn, putting on a fake, cheesy model pose and flashing gold, star-shaped clips in my hair and a matching dusting of gold on each cheekbone.

"And now for Tilda Gilmore!" Rachel announced.

Oh, yes … after going very quiet and sloping off home this morning, Tilda had surprised me by turning up tonight. "I don't care about whether Si invited me to the party or not – I just want to hang out with all of you, if that's all right," she'd said. I didn't *totally* believe her; the part about not caring about Si, I mean. But I was just glad she'd decided to come along, and hoped she wouldn't spend too much time looking over at him longingly.

"Very dramatic!" announced Dad, as Tilda did a little curtsy with her tutu, and blew a kiss with her metallic purple lips.

"Now, all of you have a good time, but remember to stick together. And if there's—"

"—any sign at all of any booze or anything, leave straight away," I said, finishing Mum's sentence/lecture in the same way as Rachel did when her mum was fussing.

It's just that my parents had already had this conversation with me earlier, and I'd said "yes", "no", "I understand" and "I promise" (and really meant it) and I didn't want them dragging it all up again in front of my friends.

"And don't be home too late," Dad chipped in, getting up to see us to the door as he noticed me starting to usher my friends out. "Oh, and wait there, Stella – I wanted to give you something..."

I bit my nail, wondering if it was a DIY tracking device or handmade alcohol detector he'd knocked up this afternoon. As I bit and wondered, I felt the furriness of Peaches wend in a figure-eight around my bare ankles.

"There we go!" said Dad, handing me a torch. "It'll be dark on that rocky path coming back up from Sugar Bay, later."

"Thanks," I replied, shoving it in my bag. "Right, let's go!"

My stomach did a quick loop-the-loop, the way it always did when I was either *very* excited or about to be sick. As Frankie had pointed out in her text, we were going to a party, on a beach, with Si Riley and his mates, and that was very cool indeed. Even if Si Riley wasn't exactly expecting five out of six of us to turn up.

And with a shower of popcorn, as Bob gave himself a shake, we were on our *very* excited way…

As it turned out, Si Riley didn't mind the fact that Amber had brought all of us along as her own personal gatecrashers. There were three reasons for this:

1) Si didn't care 'cause the party hadn't anything to do with him – it had been the idea of a bunch of the surfers who'd taken over both our bays (public and hidden away) this week.

2) There were so many people milling about on the beach (about thirty or more) that we'd hardly seen anything of Si anyway.

3) The only time we *had* caught a glimpse of him, he'd been sitting basking in the last of the day's sunshine with a bottle of cider in his hand, and was maybe a bit too interested in *that* to notice us.

My stomach did another quick loop-the-loop, as I glanced over towards the big bonfire of driftwood that people were enthusiastically adding to. At that second, it dawned on me that my stomach didn't *only* feel that way when I was very excited, or about to be sick. It also happened when I felt like things were kind of out of control.

And right now, watching the fire get bigger, the cans being passed around, and the boisterous yelling and dancing that was going on, it made me in the mood to surprise my parents by arriving home *much* earlier than I'd promised them I would...

Maybe I'd have left already, if it hadn't been for the fact that I didn't want to spoil things for my friends, or leave Sugar Bay and Joseph's house behind to these outsiders; these partying surfer lads in particular, who seemed oblivious to the grand building behind them, as their drunken dancing sent shadows from the fire bounding on the paint-chipped walls and boarded-up windows.

Trying to ignore the slight panicky sensation in my stomach, I reached into my bag and took out the card Elize Grainger had drawn. Holding it up in the rich pinky red light of the setting sun, I saw that – just as I'd hoped – I was standing in round about the right position in the garden that Elize must've been when she'd sketched this view of the house. There might have been no dancing dragonflies, and the present wooden boards across the windows were a lot uglier than the original, velvet-draped windows, but the ball of fiery, setting sun behind it was certainly the same.

"What are you doing?"

Tilda made me jump, silently stepping up in front of me in that strangely dreamy, orange light before duskiness sets in. Her twinkly greeny-blue eyeshadowed eyes stared unsettlingly at me. A minute ago, she'd gone on a hunt in the overgrown garden to find a bush big enough to have a wee behind, accompanied(ish) by me and Rachel.

"Just checking out this," I said, flipping the card round for her to examine. "I didn't see where you went just now – I thought you were lost!"

Oops.

As soon as I said that, I suddenly realized that we'd all been at this party for about twenty minutes now, and *already* I'd broken two out of three promises to my parents: I *hadn't* left the minute I saw alcohol (and there was plenty here, by the looks of it), and I *hadn't* made sure we'd stuck together (Amber had decided she should go and find Si and at least thank him for the invite; Megan, TJ and Bob were all down by the water's edge, watching some of the surfers showing off on their boards).

The broken promise thing made me feel bad, but it wasn't as if I was the *only* person doing something their parents might not approve of…

"Mum! *Why* do you have to call me every five

minutes? OK, half-hour ... whatever!"

Rachel was having one of her usual tetchy phone conversations with her mother.

"I *told* you, I'm at the beach."

Rachel didn't bother mentioning that it was the beach at Sugar Bay, not the main beach at Portbay.

"*Nothing*. I mean, we're just hanging out, watching some surfers."

Well, that much was true.

"I don't know ... just a while! We'll chat a bit and have some chips, I s'pose!"

On the main beach, the chip shop stayed open late, tempting wafts of fried, salt'n'vinegary foods floating out of the open door. In Sugar Bay right now, there was no food to be had, but plenty of beer, judging by all the slightly drunk, very noisy older teenagers fooling around on the sands.

"No, I'm *not* cold, Mum," Rachel said wearily.

She wasn't. Apart from the last saffron-coloured rays beating down, we had the big, crackling bonfire at hand. (Speaking of that, I heard a few loud, chest-vibrating splintering sounds going on – someone must have thrown on some pretty big hunks of dry, snapping driftwood on the fire.)

"*No!* You *don't* have to come and pick me up

later! I'll walk home with the others when we're ready to leave. Bye."

Tilda stared at Rachel quizzically.

"Why didn't you just tell your mum where you were?" she asked.

"Because she *thinks* I've got epilepsy, and is *sure* I'll have a seizure, even though I've only passed out twice and both times were ages ago!"

Tilda said nothing. Had she been around the time at the lido or at the café when Rachel had passed out? Maybe. Or maybe Si had said something. Either way, perhaps that's why she didn't seem too surprised, and tactfully changed the subject.

"Listen, come and see what I found under a bush over here!"

As Tilda began striding over tangled, thorny rose bushes intertwined with ivy, Rachel pulled a face at me.

"We're not going to step in your *wee*, are we, Tilda?" she asked, with revulsion in her voice.

"Different bush," said Tilda, matter-of-factly. "Anyway, check this out!"

Going down on her haunches, Tilda raised a large, low-slung branch and pointed.

"What is it?" asked Rachel warily, as if she expected to see a dead body lurking in there.

Well, I guess there was something to that.

"Gravestones," I told her, spotting the row of tiny, higgledy-piggledy carved stones lined up against the remains of a rusted, hidden set of railings. Quickly, I took the torch out of my bag and shone it on them.

"Gravestones?!" squeaked Rachel. "We're standing above *dead* people?"

She took a cat-like leap back before I could say more.

"I don't think they're *people*, exactly," I said.

"What d'you mean?"

Rachel slowly hunkered down beside us, a respectful/fearful metre or so behind me and Tilda.

"People don't tend to have names like 'Bobbins', 'Lucky', 'Lord Fluffy' and 'Duke'," said Tilda.

"What, they're like ... *pets'* graves?"

Rachel had to be right – these ten or twelve stones must've been for beloved pets – beloved pets of the Grainger family, and even Elize when she lived here on her own as an older lady. They were all touchingly simple, with just the name and year they died ("Nelson, died 1848", "Smudgie, died 1868"), except for one that had an old, dust-encrusted vase embedded in the ground in front of it and the inscription "Marmalade, who befriended me when I first moved here as a young girl. Died 1843".

It didn't occur to me as I read it in my head, that someone was reading it aloud, just a heartbeat behind.

"'...Died 1843'. Hey, *you* know lots about Elize Grainger, Stella. How old would she have been then?" asked Tilda.

"Same age as me, thirteen," I said, quickly doing the maths.

"And she had a ginger cat too, same as you, Stella!"

Tilda smiled that same intrigued smile she'd beamed our way when we'd all got spooked by the wind and nothing else in the churchyard in town the other day.

"How do you know that cat was ginger?" Rachel frowned, distracting me from the thundering in my chest at the newest coincidence.

"Um, because the clue's in the name; people don't *usually* call black and white cats 'Marmalade'," Tilda said, with a touch of amiable sarcasm.

I had a mad thought for a second. It was a mad thought that probably popped into my head because I was here at Joseph's house, feeling strange and sad and sentimental about the people who'd lived here and the fact that no one at this party except me and my friends probably knew or cared that the bulldozers were due to move in on Monday. Anyway, *here* was my stupid mad thought, a thought that no one in their right mind would even consider: I'd inherited the spirit of Elize's pet. Peaches was a *ghost*...

Just as the sensible left-hand side of my brain came charging in, pointing out that *no* cat that fat and scruffy – a cat who could wolf down a can of sardines and a custard cream for afters in nine seconds – could be in any way a wafty, serene spirit, we heard a frighteningly loud BANG! BANG! BANG! followed by a crashing CRACKKK!

Startled, the three of us clambered to our feet and looked in the direction of the house and the noise that we'd just heard.

"Stella! Up here!" yelled TJ from an upstairs window. "They've broken in! They're taking off all the boards!"

I don't think either the right- or left-hand sides of my brain got a look in – my feet took over, bounding me over the rustling plants and vines, around the side of the building to where the front door had been flung open. I carried on on automatic pilot, flying up the stairs, as people I didn't know came down with bundles of flat wood – used by the council for the express purpose of boarding up the windows.

As I weaved between bodies stomping here, there and downwards, I knew, even in the half-light, where I was headed: the room that had belonged to Elize as a little girl. The room where Joseph had carved their names (*"friends for eternity"*) on the window sill, when they were children.

"Isn't it great!" yelled TJ, as we stumbled into the room, to the sound of someone hauling off another chunk of wood from the formerly blinded window. "They're letting the house be alive again!"

Amber and Megan, standing close by with Bob, swapped slightly uncomfortable glances.

"TJ," said Megan, the upturned curls in her blonde hair now drooping, "I think they're just stealing the wood for the bonfire…"

I glanced at the window sill – and my heart fell two floors when I saw it was gone; gone for firewood? And then I noticed the neatly sawn cuts on either side, and realized the museum had done what they'd promised and sent someone to remove it for their permanent exhibition. Thank goodness…

"Whatever..." said Tilda, who'd followed me into the room, along with Rachel. "It's just a chance for us to be in here again, and maybe try and pick up some feelings or messages from Elize or Joseph!"

Rachel stopped dead and turned to Tilda.

"You *are* a witch, aren't you, Tilda Gilmore?" she said bluntly.

Me, TJ, Megan and Amber; we all held our breath and waited to hear what Tilda had to say. But she didn't immediately say anything ... mainly because she was giggling.

"Oh, I'm a witch, am I? I *wish*! How do you work *that* one out, Rachel?"

"'Cause of what you just said," Rachel blustered defensively. "And ... *and* 'cause we saw you going into that pyschic's place – that Madame Xara's – this week!"

"Well, yeah, I'd *love* to get some kind of message from Elize or Joseph, but that doesn't mean I know it's going to happen!" Tilda shrugged. "And Madame Xara – she's my auntie June; well, my *sort*-of-auntie, since she's a friend of my mum's. She works in the cheese shop too, and Mum asked me to pop in to her tarot shop or whatever it's called to collect a cheese platter."

"A *cheese platter*?!" I said, feeling a little giggle wriggling in my chest. "What's a cheese platter?!"

Whatever it was, it didn't sound too psychic...

"Lots of cheese!" Tilda grinned back at me. "Mum had ordered it for her Book Group meeting that night!"

I guess the question was answered, in a cheesy way. But then I realized I had *another* one about that same day...

"Yeah, but Tilda; when you were at Madame Xara's door, you stared straight over at me," I said. "D'you remember? It really spooked me out – as if you could read my thoughts..."

"Stella," Tilda said, and giggled again. "I need *glasses*. I can just about make out what's happening across a road, but I'd never be able to see from the doorway of Auntie June's shop right across the road and all the way down to the – Oh, *wow*!"

The "Oh wow" – it was reserved for the white, clown-footed bird that had just flap-flap-flapped its way on to the window sill.

"This guy turns up *all* the time!" said Tilda in surprise, pointing to the psycho seagull, staring cross-eyed at us all.

"He used to stalk me!"

TJ automatically took one step back, as if he

was worried the psycho seagull might swoop in on him for old times' sake.

"Really?" said Tilda. "Y'know, I felt like he was following me too – but in a *good* way – a couple of weeks ago."

The psycho seagull flapped his wings a little, opened his beak in a yawn, and stared at us.

"He was the only one who saw what I did…"

Tilda suddenly looked surprised, as if she hadn't planned on saying that last bit out loud.

"What did you do?" Megan asked her nosily.

Tilda started blushing through her pale make-up. "Well…" she began, glancing in Megan's direction, "I let the air out of a bouncy castle. Si was in there snogging your sister, Megan."

"*You* did that?" Megan gasped, remembering, same as we all did, how Si and Naomi got nabbed by Megan's parents as the out-of-bounds bouncy castle deflated all around them.

"Umm … yep," said Tilda simply, twisting a finger round a chunk of black bobbed hair.

"Hey, I guess if you were a *real* witch," said Rachel, "you could've cast a spell on Megan's sister and turned her into a warthog or an anteater, or something."

"Yeah, well, the next best thing was to sneak round the back of the bouncy castle and switch off the vacuum cleaners that pumped it up – and get the hell out of there. But the weird thing was, the whole time, *this* little guy was flapping over my head –"

Tilda pointed to the bird in the window, currently scratching his chest with his beak.

"– and I thought he was a bit like my guardian seagull angel or something. Well, a guardian angel with a really squawky voice and strange taste in food. Do you know he really likes candyfloss? He flew down and pinched a whole bag from me once and –"

Tilda stopped. She told me later it was because she'd seen my face, all white and shocked in the half-light, as if I'd seen a ghost. But I hadn't; I thought Bob had. Just like the time in the churchyard, his dopey eyes had begun to follow something that wasn't there. And the something that wasn't there stopped right by Rachel, who none of us noticed had turned silent and shivery and white.

"Clouds..." Rachel muttered, with her brows in a frown and her eyes tight shut.

"Is she having an epileptic fit?" gasped Tilda, stricken-faced.

"No, it's not a seizure – it's the *other* thing that sometimes happens to her," I said quickly, hurrying towards Rach. "Sometimes she sees, well, *stuff*..."

How weird that Rachel was accusing Tilda of being a witch a minute ago, when she was the only one of us with a hint of spooky powers.

"Too many clouds..." Rachel muttered again, her eyes flipping open and suddenly staring towards the doorway – where Si Riley stood open-mouthed, staring in disbelief first at his sister and then at Tilda (he must've followed us here and heard every word of her confession) and back at Rachel again.

"Rachel! *Rachel?* What's up with her?" he said in a slightly slurring panic, rushing over to her. "What's she on about? Why does she keep saying 'clouds'?!"

But the end of Si's sentence was mostly drowned out by Bob barking.

"WOOOF! WOOOOOF! WOOOOOOOOF! WU-WOOOOOOOF-OOOF!!!!!" the hairy Alsatian yelped, jumping agitatedly back and forth at Si Riley.

Or rather, the billowing clouds of smoke hurtling out of nowhere down the corridor behind him...

"What is it?" asked Si, swirling round to see what we were gasping at.

And instantly he got it.

Whatever Si had been drinking with his mates, he seemed to sober up fast.

"I *told* them not to put that stuff on the bonfire..." he muttered, letting go of Rachel since she seemed to be as still as a statue, and hurrying over to the doorway to assess the situation.

"What stuff? Who?" I wanted to ask, but there didn't seem to be time. And it was pretty obvious what the answer to one of those questions was; this disaster, this bonfire that had somehow set the tinder-dry house on fire ... it *had* to be the fault of the surfers. Who else would be so thoughtless and stupid?

"It's getting worse... How are we going to get out of here?" Amber asked in a teeny-tiny, scared voice.

The smoke was billowing closer to the room we were in – with a sickly smell and a distant crackling in the background – and a wave of pure, white panic rippled around the room.

"Rachel!" I heard Tilda shriek.

She and TJ reached out and caught Rachel on the way down, before the juddering and shaking of her third ever seizure crashed her on to the bare, hard floorboards.

There's probably never a great time to realize you really, truly are epileptic (no matter how much you've been in denial about it) but having it proved while an old house is going up in flames around you probably isn't what you'd call perfect timing.

"What are we going to do?" I heard Amber's thin, terrified voice cry out.

"Pile out here?!" suggested Megan, running over to the gaping window and sending the psycho seagull flapping off.

"No way – it's a HUGE drop!" I said, rushing over and judging the jump. "And there're a bunch of old railings down there we could land on!"

The lack of suggestions hung in the room like the encroaching smoke.

What *were* we going to do?

How were six of us, a dog and a girl in the middle of a seizure going to get out of here?

The quick way down was long, dangerous and sharp, and the smoke-blanketed corridor leading out of the room seemed a sure route to the heart of the fire...

Swoosh...

I might have put it down to the hot waves of smoke swirling into the room, but I recognized that warm, furry figure-of-eight sensation around my ankles – even if there didn't seem to be anything there. Then it moved off.

Glancing around at floor level, I anxiously looked around for Peaches. Nothing.

Or so I thought at first, frantic glance.

Anyone else might have thought it was a trick of the sun-setting light – or the first true glimmers of the flames – but I could *just* make out Peaches' ginger tail disappearing down the corridor, faintly visible in the stealthy greyness.

"*This* way! We can still get out *this* way!" I called out, urging my friends towards the smoke.

"Are you *kidding*, Stella?!" I heard someone, or maybe a couple of someones say.

"Just hold your breath, keep down and *run*!" I ordered, gratified to see Si start to help TJ and Tilda manoeuvre Rachel forward, while a blur of the others followed on behind.

We travelled a few choking, blinding metres, in search of the top of the grand stairway.

And then I found it, too fast...

"Help!" I yelped, as my foot stepped on to nothingness and I struggled to keep my balance.

But the words lodged in my stifled throat, and a deeper, cloying darkness started to descend in my head – just as several pairs of disembodied muscly arms reached out of the gloom towards us...

Chapter 19

Places, traces and faces...

"Watch this!" said TJ's little sister excitedly, waving her hands around and casting a looky-likey shadow puppet. "I'm making a beautiful flutterby!"

Butterfly, flutterby, dragonfly ... whatever it was supposed to be, Ellie's efforts were very sweet.

"Looks like a sausage with wings," said TJ, as he lazily put his feet on Bob's broad, hairy back and stared at Elize Grainger's gravestone.

Elize Grainger's gravestone.

I wasn't scared to be there this time; just comforted.

A week-and-a-bit ago, when me, TJ and Tilda had got spooked, it was either just a case of a dopey dog (i.e. Bob) staring at speckles of dust, or an intuitive animal (i.e. Bob, again) who'd spotted – like the librarian Mr Harper said – a strange trace of someone who wasn't quite ready to disappear yet.

And maybe I was starting to believe in traces, whatever they were. As I sat there with my friends in the churchyard, all of us hunkered down on a patch of ivy squashed flat by TJ's stamping feet (another, inventive version of a crop circle), I decided that maybe the sardine-eating, fat, scruffy cat I'd grown to know and love was just a trace too. A trace of a nearly two-hundred-year-old cat called Marmalade. Or maybe Peaches was the great-great-great x 100 grandson of Marmalade, and a direct descendant of the curled, pudgy furball at Elize Grainger's feet in the old newspaper photo celebrating her centenary. Who knew?

Whatever Peaches was or wasn't, I missed him. I hadn't seen a ginger hair of him since the fire...

"Remember when the photographer took this?" said Tilda, opening a page of the latest issue of the *Portbay Journal*. "Didn't you just *love* it when he told us to smile?!"

There we all were, posed in front of a tangle of rambling roses. The overgrown garden was all that was left of Joseph's house – the fire had made the driftwood-dry timbers burn up and vanish in a puff of blackened dust by the morning. There was practically nothing left to see, and certainly nothing left to hammer and bulldoze.

"Yeah, 'Smile, kids – you nearly died!'" TJ laughed, mimicking the newspaper photographer.

I tried to laugh too, but one week on and the smoke inhalation still felt like the rawest, you-swallowed-broken-glass throat infection you could (not) wish for.

"You all right, Stella?" asked Rachel, all concerned.

Forget *me*, for a second; *Rachel* was all right. After that last seizure, the hospital had finally decided on some medication that should keep her epilepsy under control. They told her she might grow out of it, or she might not, but now that Rachel knew that – touch wood – she wasn't going to have any more unexpected seizures (or weird psychic turns) she'd been a lot less uptight and sarcastic, and a lot more relaxed.

I never thought I'd say it, but I kind of missed her sarky humour, though...

"I'm fine," I croaked hoarsely, nodding, and taking the *Journal* from Tilda to flick through.

When I'd first moved to Portbay, the local paper might as well have been written in Tilda and Si Riley's special code, for all that the stories they printed meant to me. But on every page of this edition was something I was somehow connected with. On the front page, there were the surfers –

heroes of the hour who'd stormed back and forth into the house, pulling out everyone trapped inside – their last rescue mission getting all of us outside to safety. (Surfers ruled – I'd never call even the pudgiest among them a cross between a seal and overcooked bread dough ever again…)

Then there was the saga of how the bonfire got out of control… Two of Si Riley's drunk mates had found an old can of oil and thrown it on to "really get it going". (Si didn't seem to be hanging out with them so much – he'd preferred to have his lunch-breaks with Tilda lately.)

On page three was our photo, and the whole thing about Rachel having a seizure at the height of the fire ("Near-Tragedy As Teen Collapses"), followed over the page by the happier story of the new-look Hot Pepper Jelly café, with a beaming Phil and a pretty, wide-eyed Amber by his side.

And next week's issue promised to be crammed full of *more* articles I was somehow personally linked with. Jane the reporter had told me that all the publicity had made the holiday property developers step in and promise to keep the garden of Joseph's house (and pet cemetery), as a memorial. They'd pledged money for gazebos and benches and whatever, and the *Portbay Journal* were starting up a new fund-raiser to top it up. (Sometime this week, I was going to cash my fifty pound cheque from Rachel's mum and put the money towards the cause.)

Jane had been pretty excited to hear about Elize's hidden-away grave, and said the paper was planning to do something on that too.

Then of course there was this afternoon's photo session, in Portbay Museum, with the newly saved and renovated chandelier in place in the replica of the Grainger family ballroom. I was meeting Mum there – Jane said they wanted to get us both to pose beside it. (Yes, my mum – in fact both my parents – were amazingly still speaking to me after last Saturday's drama. They might have been angry with me for getting myself into a bad situation, but after the inevitable lecture, they'd spent the last week permanently hugging me.)

"Hey, how long have we got before Stella's next burst of local fame?" TJ asked, glancing round for anyone who had a watch.

He'd lost his in the frantic scramble to get away from the burning building.

"Half an hour," I croaked, suddenly reminded of coming to, down on the beach, and seeing the flames lapping at the empty windows.

The way that Joseph's house had gone was shocking, fast, and final, but it didn't upset me any more, 'cause I realized it *had* to be better than the alternative: the ripping and bashing apart of the planned demolition. I was sure Elize would have preferred it that way...

"Listen, let me put some make-up on you before you get your photo taken," said Rachel, frowning as she touched my cheek. "You can *still* see the love bite Jamie gave you, just faintly."

"It's *not* a love bite!" I croaked, like an indignant frog with a bad cold.

"Yeah, but it does *look* like a love bite, though!" TJ said, looming into my face with a cheeky smile.

"TJ! *Gerroff*!!" I yelped, pushing him with one hand and pulling myself away by grabbing hold of a mound of ivy by Elize Grainger's grave.

"What – are you wishing I was giving you the kiss of life again, Stella?" TJ grinned at me.

Good grief... As I'd drifted back to consciousness last Saturday evening, I realized I was being kissed awake. "TJ!" I'd yelled, my muddled head switching to the Emergency Kiss (i.e. the only other kiss I'd ever had). Course it hadn't been TJ – it was a hulking, twenty-year-old surfer doing his first-aid best and trying to give me the kiss of life. It hadn't felt funny at the time, but as soon as the danger was past and the black humour kicked in, my friends had never let me live down the fact that

I'd called out TJ's name.

"Bob! *Bob!* TJ – would you tell your stupid dog to stop destroying stuff!" shouted Rachel, as Bob started scrambling his strong-clawed paws worryingly close to where my left-hand had grabbed hold of the ivy.

"Maybe he's looking for buried treasure? Like a pot of gold at the end of the rainbow?" Ellie smiled, as Bob paid no attention to anyone – least of all TJ, and scratched a jumble of vines away … leaving a darkened, moss-edged gravestone peeking out into the first daylight it had seen in decades.

"'Jos– Joseph Gr– Grainger'," I began to read, hesitating due to moss overgrowth rather than stammering.

"Oh, *wow*…" whispered Tilda, gently moving Bob away and taking over ivy-shifting duty.

"'Born 1830, Barbados. Died 1905, Portbay, Aged 75 years.'"

My heart was thumping. Joseph might have lived in that country village, but he'd spent his last years here in Portbay, which tied in with the dedication on the bench in the park. And what had Mrs Sticky Toffee said when I'd talked about going to Somerton to find traces of Joseph? "There's no place like home…"

She'd been right. I didn't need to look any closer to home to find his last resting place – the Grainger family plot – and the last clues about where Joseph's life had led him.

"'Husband to the late Grace Barnes, father to Letty Harding, grandfather to Violet Duggan –'"

Violet! I whispered silently to myself, automatically thinking of the card that was now under glass in Portbay Museum.

"'– and great-grandfather to Miss Mary Duggan. Also life-long friend to Elize Grainger of Sugar Bay – 'friends for eternity.'"

Never mind pounding; my heart was squishing so hard at the idea of Joseph and Elize being friends, long after they were master's daughter and servant boy, that I thought I might start crying there and then. The proof wasn't just in the closeness of this headstone, but in two lives entwined, as made obvious by the lovingly drawn card for Joseph's granddaughter Violet's birthday. Elize might never have married, but her token adoptive family was obviously Joseph's.

"Miss Mary Duggan – that's my old neighbour!" gasped Tilda, tracing the final name with her finger. "Remember I told you, Stella?"

She turned to face me, dark-rimmed eyes wide with excitement.

"That painting of Joseph at the museum. It used to hang in Miss Duggan's front room. I saw it when I was little! I can't believe her name is carved here!"

Of course – the woman's name was on the "bequeathed by" plaque, I remembered now.

"Wow, I can't believe Miss Duggan was connected to… Well, to all this!" Tilda laughed in delight, wafting her hand at the elegant gravestones. "Y'know, what I remember about her most was how she never wore anything except this old green raincoat and wobbly pink hat, no matter what the weather was like!"

Wham! went the rippling thunder of realization in my chest.

"I *know* her! That's Mrs Sticky Toffee!" I gabbled. "She's this old lady I talk to all the time…!"

"But… But Miss Duggan died a couple of years ago, Stella," said Tilda.

As I looked from Tilda's confused face to TJ and Amber and Rachel's blank expressions, I wished that Megan was back here again, to say something silly, offer to do a handstand, or lighten the mood – whatever.

Thank goodness for Ellie's sweet little voice, singing "Somewhere Over the Rainbow" as she collected dandelions and tossed them joyfully into the air close by.

I was about to open my mouth and say that it wasn't just *me* who saw Mrs Sticky Toffee, but my cat, my brothers and the local librarian. And then I remembered that it was the librarian Mr Harper who'd mentioned traces in the first place, and who'd said that children and animals see them more than others.

But I didn't say any of that to my friends, because I knew that it didn't matter. Whether she was a ghost, or a "trace", or another apple-green raincoat and meringue-pink hat wearing, lovely, *mad*, old lady, Mrs Sticky Toffee had been the one to help me feel most at home here in the new home town that I tried so hard to hate at the beginning of summer.

And she – as well as Peaches and the psycho seagull – had helped me find the best bunch of friends a girl-who-thought-she-was-destined-to-be-lonely could ever have.

"Must be a different old dear – Portbay's full of them." TJ shrugged.

"Must be." I nodded, though I didn't *really* think there was much chance of two elderly women choosing the same nuts, year-round outfit.

"Are you *sure* you're OK, Stella?" asked Rachel, with her new-found and slightly uncomfortable sense of empathy.

"Absolutely," I said, spotting a familiar figure on a bench over by the main churchyard path.

He spotted me too, stopping his vital bottom-licking ablutions to give me a neon-green wink.

"Hey, anyone fancy going to the Hot Pepper Jelly for an ice cream before the museum?" suggested TJ.

"Sure," I croaked, getting to my feet. "But if we pass any shops on the way, I've got to get some sardines and custard creams." (I had a funny feeling that a longish-lost cat might be jumping through my window and purring on my bed tonight.)

"Yuck – don't fancy *that* much for my tea!" joked TJ, stretching up to his not-very-full height. "C'mon, Bob!"

Bob, wearing a pair of strawberry hair clips and a touch of glitter gel in his tail, lolloped up so enthusiastically that he sent me flying into the arms of my laughing friends – and I couldn't think of a time I felt weirder, or happier…

From:	Frankie
To:	*stella*
Subject:	Top code, actually!

Hi Stella!

The coded letter you sent – I got all the girls together, and Parminder solved it in twelve minutes! (But she would – she's *such* a brainbox.) So yeah, looking forward to seeing you at half-term too!

Everyone's mad on the idea of code, by the way. Neisha says she's going to write her diary using that secret alphabet from now on, so her mum can't ever read it! Eleni's been using it to pass me notes in class, which is a laugh. Lauren says she doesn't get it, though (doh!).

So you can tell your freaky mate Tilda that she's started a new craze. Speaking of freaky ... it seriously gave me the shivers when I read that last attachment you sent, about Mrs S-T. Is that for real, what Tilda said about her being dead? Or have you seen her again round town? Your head must be mush thinking about all that stuff.

But never fear, Dr Frankie has the perfect prescription for a Bad Case Of Small Town Weirdness – seven days of real life in London with us, your old buddies!! Hurrah for your Auntie V and her invitation, and see you at half-term…

Miss you ☹, but M8s 4eva ☺!

Frankie xxx

PS That park where the photo was taken of your Nana and her boyfriend Eddie… I just looked it up in Mum's A–Z map like you asked, and I'm pretty sure it's called Victoria Park. So I'm guessing that's where we're going when you come down? Just promise me that this history trail isn't going to be as spooky as the one in Portbay, or I might have a heart attack on you…

Want to know more...?

Meet the sparkly-gorgeous Karen McCombie!

⭐ **Describe yourself in five words. . .**

Scottish, confident, shy, calm, ditzy.

⭐ **How did you become an author-girl?**

When I was eight, my teacher Miss Thomson told me I should write a book one day. I forgot about that for (lots of) years, then when I was working on teen mags, I scribbled a few short stories for them and suddenly thought, "Hmmm, I'd love to try and write a book . . . can I?"

⭐ **Where do you write your books?**

In the loft room at the top of our house. I work v. hard 'cause I only have a little bit of book-writing time –the rest of the day I'm making Playdough dinosaurs or pretend "cafés" with my little daughter, Milly.

⭐ **What else do you get up to when you're not writing?**

Reading, watching DVDs, eating crisps, patting cats and belly dancing!

Check out Karen's super-cool website!

karenmccombie.com

For behind-the-scenes gossip on Karen's very own blog,
fab competitions and photo-galleries,
join her website of loveliness now!

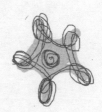